RED-HANDED DEATH

Edge tensed himself, readied the rifle for snap shooting, and lunged out of his cover. He didn't see the lance, but he heard its hissing approach from the dark and flung himself into a rolling dive. The lance powered into the rock less than three inches from his leg, spitting tiny fragments.

A brave dropped down toward him from an overhang, knife raised at the start of a swinging thrust. His painted face was twisted with a grin of triumph. Edge was on his back, the barrel of the Winchester momentarily trapped under his thighs. He released his grip on the weapon, threw himself into another roll, and landed on his feet, bringing up the lance in a powerful drive. The brave tensed, ready for the killing thrust. As the lance sank into his flesh, he screamed, filling the entire world with the sound destined to continue for eternity. His eyes bulging with shock and terror, he crumpled to the ground.

Edge grinned coldly into the pain-twisted face and drove the lance deeper. "Bad way to check out," he hissed, scooping up his rifle and the brave's knife. "Should have stayed with the reservation."

The Edge Series

EDGE

SIOUX UPRISING

by
George G. Gilman

PINNACLE BOOKS • NEW YORK CITY

EDGE: SIOUX UPRISING

Copyright © 1974 by George G. Gilman

All rights reserved, including the right to reproduce
this book or portions thereof in any form.

A Pinnacle Book, published by special arrangement with
New English Library, London.

ISBN: 0-523-00360-9

First printing, June 1974
Second printing, October 1974
Third printing, October 1975

Printed in the United States of America

PINNACLE BOOKS, INC.
275 Madison Avenue
New York, N.Y. 10016

For R. H. for taking care of Edge's hard life

CHAPTER ONE

It was early spring in the Dakotas and weak sunlight sparkled on the breeze-ruffled surface of Spear Lake. It did little to warm the ice-cold water, and the biting air drifting from out of the north protected the frost which powdered the frozen ground of the surrounding hills. So it was that the grey wood-smoke whipping from the chimney of the cabin by the lake acted as a spur to the drivers of the half-dozen assorted buggies and buckboards converging on the shore. For smoke meant a fire to warm chilled flesh: and probably steaming hot coffee to chase out the cold which seemed to penetrate bone deep.

Five of the drivers were ruddy-faced farmers, uncomfortable in their Sunday-best suits, tight-fitting polished boots and stiff-collared shirts decorated with bootlace ties. Beside them, pleased by the opportunity to dress in their carefully preserved finery, were the men's wives. On rear seats rode the children: as spick-and-span as their parents. Whether they shared their fathers' discomfort or their mothers' pleasure depended upon either their ages or their inclinations.

Preacher Dawson, a widower for many years and childless, rode alone in his buggy, on the trail that connected Spearville with the lake for which it was named. He reached the shoreline and halted the buggy to wait for Jed Hayhurst to bring his buck-board down the slope of the trail which snaked away through the hills to his farm, almost five miles away. That five miles, plus the four more from the lake into town, was Jed's excuse for only going to church for the christening of a new offspring.

That had meant the stern-faced Hayhurst and his thin, old-before-her-time wife had worshiped public-ly a mere five times in the past seven years. As the buckboard drew level with the buggy and stopped, Bertha Hayhurst was nursing the two youngest chil-dren on her bony knees. The other three sat stiffly erect in the rear. The woman's sparse figure was be-ginning to thicken and the preacher sighed inwardly as he touched his hat-brim to her. He judged the family would be requiring his services long before summer was out.

"Morning, reverend," Hayhurst greeted. "Nice day for a wedding."

"Every day is fine for the Lord's work," the preacher replied in the censorial tone which was a constant feature of his speech.

He was a tall, thin man with aquiline features and skin the color of fresh-made dough. The paleness of his complexion was emphasized by the clerical black-ness of his suit and frock coat which, in its turn, seemed to underscore the grubby greyness of his col-lar of office. There was not a woman in Spearville or within fifty miles of the town who was not of the opinion that it was time the preacher took a new wife to care for him.

Hayhurst ran a work-roughened hand over the stock of the Henry repeater rifle resting on the seat beside him, then nodded to the Winchester propped up in one corner of the buggy. "You reckon He's

2

working on the Sioux so we won't have no need to use these?" he asked.

"Jed!" his wife hissed in rebuke.

"We are all God's creatures," the preacher intoned. "He moves in mysterious ways and we cannot try to understand His every act. We should only pray for His protection when certain of His creations fail to follow the path of righteousness."

He slapped the reins over the back of the horse and drove his buggy on ahead along the shoreline towards the cabin.

"And carry a rifle to blast the cruds if they hit the path of war," Hayhurst muttered, setting the buckboard moving in the wake of the buggy.

"Jed—the children!" his wife chided.

On the other tracks from the out-lying farms, which all linked with the main trail into town at the side of the lake, the rest of the adult wedding guests also experienced more than a little anxiety tempering their anticipation of the nuptial celebrations. Jim Striker drew his buggy alongside George Cain's wagon and there was a rapid exchange of polite greetings.

"Heard the Injuns burned out a spread east of Deadwood couple of days ago," the fair-headed Striker said.

Cain was embarrassed when his wife put her hand under his, but he did not pull it away. He was prepared to allow public displays of trust and affection until they had been married a full year. "Heard that, too," he replied. "And that another bunch massacred an army patrol up to the north of here."

Striker nodded sagely. "Story goes the whole Sioux nation's fixing to meet up at a place on the South Fork River," he supplemented.

Mrs. Cain squeezed her husband's hand tighter

3

and glanced over her shoulder. The Striker boys—ten and twelve—were listening to the exchange of scare rumors with mounting apprehension.

"Can't we just forget about Indian trouble for today?" she pleaded, shooting a sidelong glance towards Mrs. Striker and receiving a nod of agreement.

"Weddings ought to be happy occasions," Sarah Striker pointed out.

Striker was twice the age of his twenty-eight year-old unattractive wife, but his cynicism made him seem even older than that. "Only happy thing about today is that we'll all be together," he said solemnly. "So if the savages attack, we'll be able to give them a big dose of their own murdering medicine."

He clucked to his horse and the buggy re-started down the trail, with George Cain's buckboard lumbering along behind.

Ed Johnston, driving his wife and three children, was the first to halt his buckboard in the neatly fenced yard at the side of the cabin. Both the Johnstons nodded formally to Mr. and Mrs. Ross as they arrived and climbed down from their buggy. The sour-faced Ephraim made a move to lift his Winchester from out of the back, but his duskily handsome wife shook her head emphatically. Young Danny Ross eyed Mildred Johnston in tongue-tied surprise, marveling at the difference six months and a store-bought dress had made to a girl he remembered as a skinny, spotty-faced kid. Mildred blushed scarlet and refused to meet the boy's highly interested gaze.

"Do we go on in, or wait for the others?" Ross wanted to know.

"I think Reverend Dawson should make the introductions," Mary Johnston suggested, frowning at the Ross boy's frank admiration for her sixteen-year-old daughter. "After all, he's the only one out of all of us who's met the new folks."

This was true. The couple who were to be married that morning had arrived in Spearville only two weeks previously. The woman had put up at the Dakota Star Hotel while the man had made inquiries for a suitable spread and paid cash-on-the-line for the old McCord place: the cabin on the lake shore with its forty acres of good growing land which had lain empty and uncared for since the bank had foreclosed on the drunken old man's mortgage eighteen months ago.

When the couple had approached the preacher to ask him to marry them, it had been the Reverend Dawson's suggestion that the occasion be used to introduce the newcomers to their neighbors on the other isolated farmsteads east of town. There were few opportunities for social gatherings among the farmers and their families so, despite the bitingly cold weather and the increasing number of stories about Indian attacks in the territory, every invitation had been taken up.

At the window of the small living room of the cabin, a man and a woman watched the approach of their guests. She was a slender red-head of twenty-five, high-breasted and narrow-waisted. Her well-formed features, dominated by expressive green eyes, were just beginning to lose their girlish prettiness in favor of womanly beauty. She was dressed in a store-bought white gown, cut modestly high at the neck and nipped in only slightly at her waist so that it hinted at, rather than emphasized, her figure.

She was tall for her sex, but the height of the man at her side underplayed her stature. He stood

5

six feet three inches and had a lean look, despite the fact that he packed almost two hundred pounds of body weight. But this was mostly strong bone and supple muscle, outlined today by a dark blue New York tailored suit and sparklingly white shirt complete with a broad, conservative necktie. His clean-shaven and lightly talced face was in drastic contrast to the pale and delicate lines of that of the woman. His complexion was burnished by Latin blood and exposure to every type of weather. Against this, his light blue eyes, surveying the world coldly from under hooded lids, seemed an incongruity. But not so much as they would have done had his Swedish mother not passed on the high cheekbones, determined jawline and thin lips of a European heritage to match the eyes: to set against the skin tone and thick black hair that had come from his Mexican father.

He was the man who had come to be known as Edge. The woman at his side was named Elizabeth Day. As they waited for their wedding guests to arrive, there was nothing in their attitudes or expressions to hint at the tragic circumstances under which they had met and the violent aftermath of their meeting.* Edge, unusually well-groomed and neatly dressed, was experiencing the normal degree of apprehension for a man about to be married. Elizabeth, for her part, viewed the scene in the yard with concern for two reasons. One of these was the customary trepidation of a bride-to-be over whether she had made the right choice for a husband. And the other was caused by the fact she had arrived at the cabin unchaperoned. Such a situation would have drawn criticism in her native Philadelphia; but out here in the wilderness of the Dakotas, among

*See *Edge—Bloody Summer & Edge—Violence is Black.*

6

strait-laced country folk, it could mark her for life as a brazen woman.

"Oh my, they've all come!" she said in a hushed whisper.

Edge showed her a cold smile, of the type that curled his lips back over his teeth but failed to reach his eyes. It was one of the many things about the man which Elizabeth had vowed to herself she would change. His inability to express amusement in the conventional way—perhaps even an incapacity to feel it—had been born out of the horrors of the Civil War and the violence which had been such a large part of his life since. But she was determined the future was going to be vastly different from the past.

"Chance of free food and drink is something not many people turn down," he replied and glanced over his shoulder, across the sparsely furnished but neat and clean living room through the open doorway into the kitchen. In there, a trestle table sagged under the weight of food carefully prepared by Elizabeth and bottles Edge had bought at The Crazy Lady Saloon in Spearville.

"I don't care if they hate the food and don't touch a drop of the liquor," Elizabeth said. "Just so long as they like us."

Edge ran a scrupulously clean finger around the inside of the stiff shirt-collar, seeking relief from the unaccustomed constriction. His fingertip touched the cord attached to the pouch hanging from the nape of his neck. In the pouch was a cut-throat razor which had brought death and agony to countless men. He realized how unnecessary it was to carry the weapon on this of all days, but it had been with him so long it was almost a part of him—he would have felt naked without it.

Elizabeth drew in a deep sigh and went towards

7

the door as the final buckboard halted in the yard and the guests moved as a group in the direction of the stoop. "Here they come," she said with a tremor in her voice.

"You sound like you wished they were going," Edge replied.

She shot a glance at him and saw his eyes were no longer cold as they drank in the sight of her. "I'll be glad when it's over," she agreed.

"Me, too," he told her, his voice and expression heavy with meaning.

Elizabeth blushed, and smiled coyly. "Have patience," she chided good-naturedly.

"Poker's my game," he answered as a heavy fist rapped on the door. "You're showing a pair and I don't want any full house around when I see what you've got in the hole."

Her color deepened and she patted her hair with a trembling hand as she pulled open the door.

"Ah, good morning, Miss Day," the preacher greeted, making a valiant effort to brighten his normally solemn tone. "All ready to complete the match?"

Edge kept his voice low so that those outside could not hear what he said. "It's a game, preacher. Let's get this deal over so we can change it to stud."

CHAPTER TWO

The two Sioux braves stayed in the cover of the large expanse of spruce trees for a long time after the wedding guests had filed into the cabin. The sudden appearance of the wagons and buggies on the hill trails had surprised them and the braves whispered rapidly to each other as they watched the families and the preacher converge on the tiny house by the lake. One of the young warriors had scouted Lake Spear earlier in the week and seen just a lone man working on the old McCord place—fixing the hole in the roof, putting new glass in the broken windows and repairing the picket fence around the yard.

The word had been sent out to every Sioux in the Dakotas—hit the whiteman whenever and wherever he was vulnerable. Burn, pillage, rape and slaughter in every part of the territory. So that when the uprising took place the whites would be weakened and terrified: almost powerless to retaliate against the might of the massed Sioux nation.

But they were just two braves, decked out in feathered headdresses and with garish warpaint streaked on their faces and naked chests—prepared and well able to claim the life of a single white man. But now there were seven men in the house and the new odds of better than three-to-one against were unappealing to the braves.

So they stayed crouched among the timber which almost completely covered the rising ground behind the cabin and discussed whether to abandon their planned raid or to seek the glory of seven male scalps and the pleasure of as many women.

What finally decided them was the liquid courage drawn from a bottle of corn-juice stolen on their last raid; and the memory of the boasts they had made to the old men and squaws back at the teepees. So, after making sure their piebald ponies were securely tethered, they took final swallows of cheap liquor, tossed away the empty bottle and started silently down the open slope towards the rear of the cabin. Each carried a Winchester rifle across the front of his vividly decorated body and had a tomahawk and knife slotted through the belt of his buckskin pants.

The approach of the braves was unseen, for everyone was crowded into the small living room at the front of the cabin, listening in reverent silence to the measured tone of the preacher's voice.

"I now pronounce you man and wife," he finished, snapping closed his prayer book and hanging a broad smile on his wan face. He looked quickly around at the guests, noting the boredom of the children, the moist eyes of the women and the impatience of the men. "Mr. Hedges, you may kiss Mrs. Hedges," he announced after a suitable pause to separate the solemnity of the marriage service from this incitement to indulge lust.

Lack of composure was not one of Edge's failings. It had been, as a boy, of course. But war had transformed an immature and artless youth into a self-possessed and supremely confident man virtually overnight. And it was largely because of his composure and life-hardened ability to act coolly in all situations that he had survived the intervening years. But now, as he sensed the gazes of the guests upon him, and saw the beaming face of the preacher and the shining eyes of his brand-new wife, he experienced the full depth of discomfort into which embarrassment could sink the human mind and physical being.

He leaned forward and brushed his lips quickly over those of Elizabeth, then swung around and grinned foolishly at the onlookers. Elizabeth had warned him he would be expected to make a speech after the ceremony and a thousand things to say had run through his mind. All of them he had now forgotten and an interminable length of time seemed to pass before he spoke:

"Obliged to you folks for coming," he said hoarsely. "Miss Day—I mean my wife—and me'd be glad if you'd stay for awhile and eat with us."

There was another pause, as the expectant guests waited for him to continue. One of the two horses in the small corral behind the cabin whinnied nervously. Mrs. Hayhurst, recognizing Edge's discomfort, started to applaud. The other guests followed her cue and the sound of the clapping masked the squeals of the two horses as the braves plunged knives into the animals' throats.

The horses keeled over into death, great gouts of blood splashing to the frost-covered ground and starting to form scarlet patches of ice.

In the cabin, the new bride's and groom's neighbors pushed forward to kiss Elizabeth and pump Edge's hand. Then the women formed a chattering group around Elizabeth while the men urged Edge into the kitchen to open the imported champagne and Kentucky bourbon and rye. Danny Ross found the courage to start up a conversation with Mildred Johnston and the Reverend Dawson beamed at the couple, wondering how long it would be before he was asked to officiate out at the Johnston place. The younger children crowded into the kitchen doorway, craning their necks to see between the legs of the men—to catch a glimpse of the piles of food on the table.

"Look, a funny man!" three-year-old Matthew Johnston exclaimed, pointing towards the kitchen window.

Twelve-year-old Mark Striker glanced in the direction the toddler had indicated, but saw only the pastureland below the treeline. The Sioux brave who had chanced to peer in through the window had instantly bobbed out of sight when he saw the group of men at the table.

"Drinks coming up, ladies!" Ed Johnston announced, the prospect of so much free liquor putting him in an unusually expansive mood. "To toast the health of the happy couple."

Edge realized that he was probably supposed to serve the drinks and urge the guests to start eating. But after he had opened the first bottle the other men—the isolation of life on far-spread farms leaving them short of the proprieties—immediately set the pace for eating and drinking. He was grateful for this. For after the further embarrassment of having to stand beside Elizabeth again—like some tableau in a city museum—and be toasted by the guests, he was relieved of all formal duties.

"Tell me something," the preacher asked as Danny Ross, encouraged by his father, took a mouth organ from his pocket and began to play *My Western Home*.

12

Elizabeth was in whispered conversation with Mrs. Striker and Mrs. Cain. Edge stood in the kitchen doorway, watching the children as they attacked the food and the men downing drinks. The wedding feast was disappearing with encouraging rapidity.

"What's that?"

"How did you come to be called Edge, Mr. Hedges?"

Edge's expression changed as his mind travelled back across the blood-soaked years, recalling the shouted threat which had followed him into the night after he had sliced half a man's face away.* In the few short moments while the tall half-breed reflected on the distant past, his eyes narrowed to glinting slits and his mouth was formed into a thin, cruel line. The preacher saw the expression and felt his insides tighten with fear, sensing the evil and violence lurking beneath the surface veneer of the man.

"Long time ago and a long way from here, preacher," Edge replied softly, moderating his expression as he saw the other man's nervousness, but injecting into his voice a tone which warned against further enquiry.

"Should we call you Mr. Hedges or Mr. —"

A shrill whistle cut across the drone of the mouth organ and babble of conversation. In the next instant the front door burst open and the kitchen window shattered. Two rifles exploded as a single sound. The bullet fired by the brave at the front door tore into the back of the preacher's neck and angled upwards, bursting clear, in a spray of blood and membrane, through his right eye.

*See: Edge—The Loner.

13

In the kitchen, Cain threw himself in front of the younger Striker boy as he saw the rifle barrel zero in through the smashed window. The bullet punctured his lung and he gasped a shower of blood into the face of the screaming child.

For a second, as the Indians worked the lever actions of their rifles, drunken eyes raking over terrified faces in search of the next targets, only one man moved. The shrieks of women and screams of children merged into an ear-piercing, high-pitched sound of boundless terror as Edge launched himself across the room.

He saw the muzzle of the Indian's rifle swing around to cover him and waited a split-second for the dark-skinned finger to grow tense around the trigger. Then he went down and to the side, rolling. He knocked Mildred Johnston hard to the floor with his shoulder as the Winchester roared. The bullet ricochetting off the coffee pot on the hob gouged a long furrow along Mrs. Cain's forearm.

Edge snatched a flaming log from the fire as another rifle shot sounded in the kitchen and a man screamed. Elizabeth went into a crouch and darted across to the injured Cain woman. The brave in the doorway uttered a wailing warcry as he pumped another shell into the breech. Edge hurled the blazing log, springing to his feet. The log spun through the air, trailing smoke and dripping flaming splinters. It smashed into the Indian's face. He gave an agonized roar and staggered backwards, dropping his rifle and flinging his hands up to his face. Edge lunged across the threshold, his right hand streaking towards the back of his neck.

As he emerged into the biting cold outside, his arm swung down, hand clutching the razor. The Indian's feathers and hair were on fire, but he was still

14

on his feet. His eyes flashed hatred between scorched skin and he jerked out his tomahawk and threw it in a single, fluid action. Edge dove under the spinning weapon and thrust the razor forward and up. An agonized scream split the air just behind him. But the Indian merely gasped. The blade of the razor sank deep into his naked stomach and swept up to his throat with the ease of a twig trailed in water. Drenching blood erupted from the gigantic split in his flesh and he fell backwards, his body opened up from navel to Adam's apple.

A gun roared inside the cabin, and Edge whirled. Mary Johnston had tried to escape through the front door. Now she was in a grotesque sitting position, back resting against the frame. The entire blade of the tomahawk was buried deep in the center of her chest. Four fingers of her left hand were scattered on the ground from where she had made a futile attempt to fend off the weapon. They looked like red and white chips of wood. A gold wedding band glinted dully on one of them.

Edge leapt across her body, aware of the sudden silence which had settled over the cabin, punctured by an occasional sob or child's whimper. Elizabeth stood in the center of the room, the brave's Winchester still aimed from her shoulder. The second brave had got into the cabin, but not far. Her shot had taken him in the side of the head, splashing blood and brain matter across the kitchen wall. It had been a second too late to save Ed Johnston. The farmer's body was sprawled across the food table beneath that of the Indian. The hilt and handle of the brave's knife seemed to be growing out of Johnston's open mouth: the point had burst clear at the back and pinned the man's head to the table.

A downdraught whined into the chimney and

wood smoke billowed from the fireplace. It masked the acrid odor of exploded powder. People began to cough, then to shiver as fresh, ice-cold air streamed in through the open doorway.

"Oh, my God!" Sarah Striker screamed, rushing across the room to where her two babies gurgled happily on a spread blanket.

The other women, the trembling of shock taking over from the shivering of cold, staggered from room to room, seeking out their children. Mildred Johnston, a thin wailing sound pouring from her lips, flung herself into the kitchen and dragged the brave off her father's body. Then she pulled the knife from his mouth and began to slap his face, her hysteria rising as his staring eyes continued to show a complete lack of response.

Edge wiped the razor on his pants leg and slid it back into the pouch as he moved to the side of his wife and eased the Winchester away from her. She looked at him blankly for stretched seconds, and only then did the shock pass so that she could recognize him. She flung herself suddenly into his arms.

"I'm not going to break down, Edge," she whispered. "It's not new to me, is it? I've been through it all before—the blood and the agony and the death."

She had, but Edge knew it made no difference. He could see it in the way she held her eyes tight shut and fists clenched and could feel it in the taut stiffness of her body pressing hard against his own. And he knew it would take more than a word of agreement to prevent her pitching into hysteria. So, as he felt the first tremor shake her body, he stepped away from her. His right arm continued to encircle her shoulders. His left hand folded into a fist. Her eyes remained screwed shut, but her mouth fell

16

open to vent a scream of released shock. He pulled the punch, but clipped her hard enough on the side of the jaw to drop a dark blanket over her tormented mind. Her body sagged and he swept her easily into his arms.

Danny Ross's eyes held harsh accusation as he stared at Edge. "What you do that for, mister?" he gasped.

"Man ought to start marriage the way he means to go on, kid," the half-breed answered, heading for the door to the cabin's only bedroom. "I can't stand a noisy woman." He didn't mean it to sound harsh: he had a vague idea of injecting something into the tragic atmosphere which would at least help the boy to appreciate that life went on despite death. But Edge had learned the lesson too well himself—had lived through too much death. So much so that he had grown indifferent to it. So that the familiar cold grin curled his lips as he spoke and the utter lack of compassion in his slitted eyes combined with the mirthless smile to reveal his true attitude to the carnage the Sioux braves had brought to his wedding day. He was left alive, and so was Elizabeth. And he could feel nothing that others had died around him because there had been too many years of blood-soaked violence, draining him of the capacity to pity.

He went into the bedroom and closed the door on the reproachful stare of the boy. He laid his wife's limp form gently on the bed, then went to the fireplace and struck a match to the balled up paper among the ready-set logs. It was very cold in the room and the fire took a long time to generate heat to all the corners. During this period, Edge sat on the foot of the bed, staring out of the window at the sun-sparkled water of the lake. For the most

17

part, Elizabeth breathed evenly, as if she had slipped from enforced unconsciousness into a deep sleep accepted willingly by a mind unprepared yet to face the horrors which waking would bring. But occasionally, a low moan would escape her lips and her arms would flail weakly.

The sounds of grief and shock from the living room and kitchen gradually diminished and eventually there was just the shuffle of feet and low murmuring of occasional instructions as the dead were carried outside.

"My God, what are we going to do?" Elizabeth whispered.

Edge turned to look at her and saw she was staring up at the ceiling with wide eyes. There was a dark, painful looking bruise on her jaw, but she made no move to touch it. Her body was motionless.

"You heard what the preacher said," Edge replied. "Death hasn't parted us yet."

Knuckles rapped lightly on the door panel and Edge stood and moved across the room. He pulled open the door and Mrs. Cain lifted her tear-ravaged face to look at him.

"George is dead," she said dully. "So's the Reverend Dawson and Mr. and Mrs. Johnston. We're going into town. It'll be safer there. You and Elizabeth ought to come with us."

The living room was empty except for Mrs. Cain, who was holding her savagely gashed arm across her body with her other hand. But her eyes showed no pain. They were as dull and flat as her voice. Edge glanced over his shoulder at Elizabeth. She was still staring up at the rough planking of the ceiling, but she had heard Mrs. Cain's suggestion and sensed her husband's eyes on her.

"The Reverend Dawson spoke the words," she re-

18

minded him hoarsely. "Love, honor and obey. I made the promise."

Edge nodded and looked back at the new widow. "Obliged you thought of us," he said. "But I reckon we'll stay at home."

Mrs. Cain's numbing grief was pierced by a flicker of concern. "But the Indians?" she exclaimed. "Those two were only the start of it."

"Mrs. Cain!" Jed Hayhurst called from outside.

"You're set on staying here?"

Edge nodded. The woman looked around him and nodded to Elizabeth, then moved to the front door of the cabin.

"It would be polite to see them off, Edge," Elizabeth suggested softly.

Edge moved in the wake of Mrs. Cain. Of the white dead, only their blood remained to show where they had fallen. But the unmoving corpses of the two braves had been left where they were. He watched Mrs. Cain climb aboard the Hayhurst wagon. The dead were loaded on the Cain's buckboard, which was driven by Bertha Striker. Jim Striker drove his own buggy. The preacher's buggy, with the horse still in the shafts, was where the Reverend Dawnson had left it.

"Reckon you're a fool not to come with us," Striker growled. "But even a fool deserves a chance. Savages slaughtered your horses. Reckon the preacher wouldn't mind if he knew we left you and the wife his horse and buggy."

"Obliged," Edge replied as the drivers clucked to their horses and turned them towards the lakeshore trail which headed for town. "I'll bring both in when I come to town to fix up supplies."

"To give to the Sioux," Ephraim Ross called wryly.

"What's mine ain't easy to take away," Edge answered.

He watched his departing guests until they were clear of the yard, then turned back into the cabin. Through the open doorway of the bedroom he could see that Elizabeth was still in the same position on the bed. He went into the kitchen and lifted the dead Sioux's moccasin-clad feet to drag the body across the living room and out of the front door. He heard his wife begin to cry, very softly. He closed the door on the sound and caught hold of the second dead Indian in the same manner as the first. Then he hauled both of them across the frozen ground of the yard to the shore of the lake. Fragments of iced blood crackled and broke away from the bodies, leaving a trail.

He rested for a moment, his expelled breath looking like grey smoke in the air. Then he lifted each body and hurled it as far out into the water as his strength permitted. They splashed to their watery graves several yards from shore. Bubbles rose to mark the spots for a few moments, and the surface of the lake became calm again.

Then he squatted down, took out the makings and rolled a cigarette. The cold stream of air from the north made it difficult to strike a match. So after he had smoked the first cigarette, he lit the second from the stub of the old one. He fired four more in the same manner, and smoked them in reflective silence, unaware of the sun passing its midday peak to begin its slow slide towards the western horizon: and not hearing the sounds made by Elizabeth as she moved about inside the cabin.

For his consciousness was turned inwards, excluding all outside influences, as he considered the mistake he had made in marrying Elizabeth. If he had thought about it before, he would have realized he was one of life's losers—doomed to win only his own survival while those around him perished. That he had never considered his existence in this way before was due to the fact that it had never mattered. For while survival was the only important thing, the winning of it was paramount. But it had all been a trick of fate. All the agony and the killing had only seemed to wring him dry of emotion: in fact, all the normal human feelings had been driven into the deep storage of his heart. And there they had remained, waiting the right moment to be released by love for a woman.

Elizabeth had opened that store and Edge, confounded by the stupor with which love is able to enshroud the strongest of men, had been fooled into believing a new kind of life was being offered to him.

But it was not to be. As he straightened from his squatting position, becoming suddenly aware of how intensely cold he was, he acknowledged the certainty that he was destined to lose Elizabeth. The two Sioux braves, now resting on the bed of the lake, could have as easily killed her as the others. That they had not harmed her was just another twist of fate, designed—Edge was sure—to warn him of the futility of seeking happiness. He was supposed to suffer anguish every second of time until the fatal blow was struck. But as he turned to walk back towards the cabin, the coldness attacking his flesh was as nothing compared to that which knifed into and stayed in his mind.

As he approached the door, it was opened and Elizabeth stood there. Beyond her, the cabin was neat and spotlessly clean again. There was not a trace of the carnage to be seen and Edge realized he must have stayed out by the lake a very long time.

"Where have you been?" she asked as he stepped across the threshold, feeling the heat from the fire caress his face and body.

"Guess you could say I've been drowning my sorrows," he answered.

"You took a bottle out there?"

"Water was good enough."

She looked at him quizzically, then shrugged. "You're cold, Edge," she said, taking his hands in hers.

He stared deep into the green pools of her eyes, trying to form the words to tell her of his decision. "Clean through," he replied at length.

"Come over to the fire," she said, tugging at him gently. "Get warm."

He shook his head. "That's only good for the outside, Beth," he told her softly. "I'm death on legs. Ain't nothing can warm that out of me."

"Goodness, what are you talking about?" Elizabeth demanded.

"Killing follows me around," he answered, allowing himself to be led to the fire and letting her urge him into a padded armchair. "It never mattered before because I didn't give a damn for anyone except me. But now it's different. I'm gonna lose you, Beth. And I'd rather see you walk away from me alive than—"

"You stop that kind of talk, you hear!" she snapped, dropping to her knees in front of him and staring up into his face with imploring eyes. "Death on legs, indeed! You're no different from any other man. Except that you're the one I love."

Edge looked down at her upturned face and struggled to generate the hate that was supposed to be over the narrow dividing line from love. But he found it was not so easy as that. The coldness was

22

still a palpable force within him, but he could not direct it towards the woman kneeling at his feet.

And when she smiled suddenly, he gave up trying. Her hands went to the back of her neck and her fingers began to work busily.

"What are you doing?" he asked quickly, as he realized she was unfastening the buttons on the back of her dress.

She held the smile in place. "If you're so sure I'm going to catch something fatal from you, I don't want to go as a virgin angel," she answered easily, then laughed at the shocked expression which crossed his face. "We're married now, Edge," she reminded him. "And the preacher said something about that making it all right to satisfy our carnal desires."

Edge blinked, immediately forgetting the recent killings and the result of his long period of self-examination. Elizabeth softened her smile and rose slowly to her feet, holding the dress in place with her chin. Then, as she tilted up her head, the neckline fell away. The firm mounds of her pink-crested breasts thrust nakedly forward at his eye level. She wriggled her hips briefly and shook her arms. The dress pulled free of her wrists and fell softly to the floor about her feet. A heat much greater than that from the fire engulfed Edge's body, inside and out, as he raked his eyes over the pale nakedness of his wife. The red triangle crowning the twin columns of her slender legs held his gaze like some tangible force demanding his undivided attention. But, at the same time, a counter-force held him transfixed in the chair, unable to move.

Elizabeth's short laugh cut across the invisible ties which held Edge and his gaze swept up to her face. He saw a mischievous sparkle in her eyes.

"You said you were going to see me, so I got

ready to show you," she said, pointing across the room to where her undergarments were stacked in a neatly-folded pile on a bureau. "You're showing a flush, Edge. I'll want to see what else you've got before I know you can take me."

He had to force the words out around a lump in his throat. "I'm playing with two hands," he croaked, feasting his eyes on her rippling flesh again.

"So, why don't you use them, Edge," she urged softly, taking a step closer to him.

He rose to meet her and as she sagged against him, he lifted her in his arms. "You're ready to go for the middle?"

She nodded, and showed nervousness for the first time. "But it's a bluff, Edge. I've never played this game before," she said softly.

He carried her to the bedroom, moving sideways through the doorway. "Just take it easy, Beth," he replied as he laid her gently on the bed. "Nothing wild."

He quickly stripped off his clothing and Elizabeth's innocent nervousness increased with each new plane of his hard body which was revealed to her.

"What do I have to do to please you?" she whispered as he stretched out on the bed beside her, cradling her head in the crook of his arm as his hand cupped her breast.

"Lose something I'm glad you saved for me, Beth," he answered, his lips moving lightly on hers.

She made one final attempt to keep up the light-hearted poker analogy. "So what have you got?" The tears began to stream down her face, but no sound emerged from her trembling lips. Edge rolled on top of her and sank into her. She gasped her pain.

"A natural straight," he murmured.

24

CHAPTER THREE

For Edge and Elizabeth, the terror which had struck so tragically on their wedding day seemed to become a distant memory from the moment of their waking after they first made love. The following morning, Edge fixed the broken window in the kitchen and buried the dead horses in the corral. Elizabeth busied herself with making curtains while he attended to these chores, and when he was finished they didn't talk about what he had done.

Nor did they talk about the Indian raid in the days and weeks which followed—and there was little time to think about it, or anything else. For they filled the daylight hours with work on the spread, driving themselves so hard that at nights they fell into a deep sleep immediately after they had made love.

Edge received a gruesome reminder one morning, when the water-bloated and fish-nibbled bodies of the two braves drifted into the shore of the lake. The hardly recognizable human forms were bound together by a tangle of weeds and he buried them like that, in the soft mud of an inlet, above the waterline now that the spring sunshine had evaporated the excess of winter rain from the lake.

He considered mentioning his find to Elizabeth, but decided against it. Despite the conclusions he had drawn from his period of introspection on that bitterly cold day, his life with Elizabeth had so far proved immeasurably happy. And his wife gave every impression of sharing his joy. But each morning when he awoke, his first act was to reach out and touch her sleeping form. He recognized this as a symptom of continued distrust of the new phase in his life. And he did not want to give fate the least opportunity to attack him again. So he held his silence, fearful that Elizabeth would be reminded of his invitation for her to leave him—and take it because the reappearance of the dead braves was proof of his assertion that wherever he went and whatever he did, violence would never be far away.

So he did not tell Elizabeth about the braves in the inlet and pushed the fact into the back of his own mind, to where most of his past had been relegated. It was safe there, for he was able to draw a blind across everything that had happened to him up to the day Elizabeth had agreed to become his wife. He was helped in this by the woman, who was never moved to ask questions about his past. Just as Edge never voiced any curiosity about Elizabeth's life during the years before he met her. They merely accepted each other for what they were, choosing to ignore the circumstances which formed the character of their partner.

It was as if both had been reborn on the day of their wedding, with a new destiny: which was to love each other to the exclusion of all outside influences. A measure of their success was that Edge felt himself unburdened of his fatalistic attitude and Elizabeth discovered that her plans to alter her husband did not have to be put into effect. For Edge, born of farming stock, was able to settle back into the mold without the least difficulty: and in so doing, the taint of the killer was gradually eradicated, the ambience of violence dropping away from him in stages like discarded clothing.

Within two months, as they plowed and planted the fields, built a barn and remodeled the cabin into a house suitable for family life rather than the habitat of a drunken old-timer, Edge became a new man—to himself and in the eyes of a wife who grew to love him with greater intensity each day. Elizabeth began to call him by his given name of Josiah and eventually he thought of himself thus, rejecting Edge as a harsh-sounding *nom de guerre* that had no part in his new life. It was as if it belonged to another man entirely.

When he went to town—at first accompanied by Elizabeth and then, as rumors of a Sioux uprising diminished, on his own—the people he met addressed him either as Mr. Hedges or Joe. He never went to Spearville except for a practical reason: to return the buggy and buy a wagon and team and then to purchase supplies, farm equipment and seed. The money for these necessities of life came from the bankroll he had earned in Summer. This was kept in a secret hideaway he had discovered in the bedroom of the cabin while he was fixing a section of wall-paneling which had developed the rot. The paneling concealed an alcove to the right of the fireplace and whatever its original purpose, it had been used by old man McCord to store his supply of whiskey. There was still a dozen bottles lining two of the narrow shelves at the back of the high, narrow closet when Edge discovered the panel had hinges. It was the cheapest kind of rot gut and he emptied the raw liquor into the lake. Then he made and fixed in place a new door which blended with the rest of the wall in as clever a way as the old one. And it was behind this that he lodged the money left over after his purchase of the property.

As gentle spring gave way to a fierce summer, the stack of bills became smaller. But the spending of the money was producing results in the form of material prosperity. The cabin and its extensions were worth at least three times what Edge had paid for the property and the fields around it on three sides were richly carpeted with ripening wheat and rye.

Edge felt deservedly content and at peace with the world as he harnessed the two horse team to the buckboard in the warm sunlight of an early August day. He was going into Spearville to check on the availability of a couple of milk cows. He had already fenced off the sloping pasture that extended from the back of the wheat field to the treeline of the spruce forest behind the house and, following a discussion with Elizabeth, had decided that cows would be more useful to them than the horses he had originally intended to buy.

Elizabeth emerged from the house just as he was finishing tightening the traces to the correct tension. She wore the red and green floral-patterned dress he had bought for her on a previous trip to town—one of the few luxuries he had indulged in amid so many necessities of life. She had rebuked him for the waste of money, because the dress had been made for beauty rather than practicality. It was low cut and hugged her figure like a second skin to the waist, then flared away in the froth of many petticoats to her ankles. Hardly the gown for a farmer's wife who had no interest in even the limited social activity of Spearville. But Edge enjoyed seeing her in the dress so she wore it from time to time, during the few inactive periods in their busy life on the farm.

"Something special, Beth?" he asked, turning at the sound of her footfalls across the yard. His clear blue eyes, wide and gentle, drank in the sight of her like a young man experiencing the first nervous stirrings of love.

She smiled as she held out the hundred dollars she had taken from the hideaway. "Ten minutes after you've gone, I'll be back in grey denim," she replied. "But I'd prefer you to remember me like this in case you go into the saloon and happen to see the dancing girls."

Edge grinned as he took the money, put it in his shirt pocket and swept his wife into his arms. He kissed her gently on the lips, then looked down at the exposed tops of her breasts as they flattened slightly against his chest. "If I remember you like this, I won't even look at The Crazy Lady girls," he promised. "But if any one of them just happens to catch my eye, there's an even better memory of you I got in reserve."

From the moments preceding the consummation of their marriage, Elizabeth had never displayed modesty, false or genuine, in regard to their love-making. Now she laughed, the sound shrill and clear in the quiet morning air. "Just so long as you don't try making any comparisons, Joe."

He kissed her lightly once more, then swung up on to the seat of the buckboard. As he looked down at her the sunlight struck her red hair at such an angle that it seemed to be run with threads of gold. He could not recall when he had last seen her looking so radiantly beautiful.

"The Crazy Ladies saloon might be like heaven to some fellers," he said. "But they sure don't have any angels there."

She bobbed her body in an overplayed curtsey in

29

acknowledgement of the compliment, then trilled with laughter again. "Must be all that ambrosia I've been eating," she said.

"The guy at the grocery store told me it was canned rice," Edge answered.

"He's just got no imagination," Elizabeth countered.

"But I have," Edge said, tearing his gaze away from her upper body, its every curve faithfully reproduced by the dress. "And I better get rolling before it starts working overtime."

The laughter went out of her green eyes to be replaced by devotion. "The sooner you go, the sooner you'll be back, Joe," she said. "Take care."

"I will," he promised, and clucked to the horses, tugging on the reins so that they hauled the buckboard in a tight turn.

He drove out along the trail which curved around the shore of the lake, and didn't look back. But when he reached the far shore he glanced across the sparkling mirror of the broad sheet of water and saw that she was still standing in the yard before the cabin. He waved and she responded, then waited until he had swung away from her again, on the trail snaking between the hills towards Spearville before she turned and entered the house.

She went into the kitchen and there was enough coffee in the pot to pour herself half a cup. She took a long time to drink it, enjoying this period of deep reflection upon her happiness: marvelling at the unruffled calm which had come to a partnership created amid so much tragedy. But then sadness intruded upon her reflections, arising from the empty stillness in the house which stressed the lack of her husband's presence.

She knew how to deal with this, however: had

30

learned on the previous infrequent occasions when Edge was gone that the only way to alleviate the threat of depression which his absence brought was to throw herself into work. So she rose from the kitchen table and went out into the living room, deciding that Edge's trip to Spearville presented her with the perfect opportunity to decorate the bedroom. She had asked him to buy two cans of pale blue paint several weeks ago, without telling him why she wanted them. He had probably forgotten all about the purchase by now and her handiwork would be a complete surprise to him.

As she crossed the threshold into the bedroom she rubbed the ache in the small of her back. A bird whistled shrilly from the spruce forest above the cabin. She smiled and thought about the old adage which linked the color of blue with a boy. She realized it was a foolish whim, but acknowledged that her determination to paint the bedroom blue was strengthened by the hope that it would provide a lucky omen. She wanted desperately for the baby forming inside her to be a boy.

The bird among the trees whistled again, and she frowned. There was something derisive in the sound. But then she smiled and hummed as she prepared to start work. All her other dreams had come true and she was not going to allow any stupid bird to mar her newest hope.

CHAPTER FOUR

Spearville was not much of a town. Just a short main street with three narrower ones leading off the north side and petering out to nothing after two hundred feet or so. But, as the only settlement of more than a few buildings in a rich farm belt, it was reasonably prosperous. It had a half dozen stores stocking the essentials of life in the rugged Dakotas and one of these—Rand's Dry Goods—had a section at the rear devoted to such trifles as ladies ready-made gowns, candy-bars for the kids and even books and out-of-date magazines.

It was to this emporium of unnecessaries that Edge went after concluding his deal with the agent of a Kansas cattle-breeder. He had obtained what he considered a bargain and decided to celebrate by buying Elizabeth a present. He selected a much-thumbed and incomplete set of the works of William Shakespeare which, Mrs. Rand told him, had belonged to the late Reverend Dawson. But there was nothing within the books to reveal their last owner. In the autumn and winter evenings to come, when the weather and early darkness halted work at the farm, Elizabeth would appreciate the books.

He left the store and placed them under the seat of the buckboard. The two cows tethered to the rear eyed him balefully and swished their tails at the irritating flies which buzzed in the hot air of late morning. The two horses were content under the shade of the awning outside the store. He had intended to head straight back to the farm after concluding his business in town, but the drive in had been dusty and the frame buildings flanking the street seemed to hold the heat of many days in a closed trap.

The painted cut-out of a foaming glass of beer hung above the sidewalk in front of the saloon looked almost real, and Edge was made very aware of his dry throat as he glanced across the street.

"Come on over and take a drink."

Edge turned towards the speaker. It was the stern-faced Jed Hayhurst, who had stepped out from the barber's shop, his hair neatly clipped and his face white with talc after a shave.

"It sounds like a good idea," Edge replied.

Hayhurst nodded and the two men moved out into the sunlight, quickening their pace towards the cool-looking shadows beyond the bat-wing doors of The Crazy Ladies. There were a half-dozen men inside, four engaged in a poker game and two leaning on the bar, fanning themselves with their hats. Inside, it was not so cool as it had looked from the street and the two girls sitting near the piano were sweating as freely as the men. Salty moisture had cut furrows through the heavy make-up on their faces and there were dark stains on their dresses beneath their armpits. Edge thought fleetingly of Elizabeth's good-natured warning and the corners of his mouth turned up in a smile.

The girls' expressions had been morose, but as the two men crossed to the bar, they raised sensual looks of allure and stood up. Their bodies adopted an accentuated swaying motion as they moved be-

33

tween the tables, hands smoothing the dresses over their hips.

"Like to buy a couple of nice girls a drink, fellers?" the blonde asked.

Up close, her black roots showed. So did her age, which was at least ten years more than the twenty-five she had looked from the doorway. Her more recently rinsed partner was even older.

"Two beers," Hayhurst told the fat bartender.

"That all?"

"Obliged," Edge told him.

"I said—" the blonde began, her smile wilting.

"If you go find us a couple of nice girls, we'll consider it," Edge interrupted.

The blonde swung around to stare at the bartender, her eyes blazing with anger. "He's insulting us, Jake!" she exclaimed.

Jake was midway through pouring the second beer. He looked up at Edge, his obese frame starting to grow taut and his expression hardening. It was obvious he intended to come to the woman's defense.

For the first time in many weeks, Edge felt his facial muscles moving in such a manner that he knew his expression had become a cold grin. He caught a glimpse of himself in the mirror behind the bar and saw it—lips curled back so that they hardly seemed to exist, skin dragged smooth over cheekbones, and eyes narrowed to mere slits of glinting light.

Jake had worked behind the bar in saloons from the Mexican border to New York City and he had stayed alive by recognizing that expression as the mark of a man prepared to kill on the slimmest provocation. He finished drawing the second beer and set both foaming glasses on the bartop.

34

"Forget it, Martha," he urged. "Heat's set everyone's nerves on edge."

Edge and Hayhurst gulped half their drinks at a swallow.

"A nerve that guy's certainly got," Martha muttered petulantly.

"It's what gives me the edge, maybe," the halfbreed answered.

"Go screw yourself, mister," Martha rapsed, whirling and stomping back towards the piano, the other woman hard on her heels.

"Ambrosia, those dames ain't been eating," Edge muttered.

"Can it, feller," Hayhurst urged, noting that the other customers were showing an interest in them and anxious that his wife should not learn he had got into a saloon brawl over a couple of whores.

Edge shrugged easily and readjusted his smile to one of warm humor. "Okay, but women have got to learn I've got me a farmer's wife now. I ain't a bachelor no more."

Hayhurst finished his beer and ordered another. "What's that supposed to mean?"

"Food for thought," Edge replied, pushing forward his glass for a refill. "My brand of humor."

They sipped their new drinks, enjoying the taste rather than relishing the mere coldness of the beer. They spoke of their crops and the effect of the weather on growth; of Edge's grand plan to build up the tiny McCord place into the biggest dairy and wheat spread in the Dakotas; of Bertha's imminent confinement with what would be her sixth child; and of a rumor that a railroad spur was to be laid up to Spearville.

No mention was made of Indian trouble, for the threatened uprising had never materialized in the

35

wake of the isolated attacks of winter and spring. And stories of more recent atrocities originated from distant sources and there was no evidence to prove their veracity. Nor did the men discuss what had happened after the wedding, for a tacit understanding had been reached among those concerned that the tragedy should never be mentioned.

A new preacher had been appointed to the church at the end of Spearville's main street. Mrs. Cain had moved back east to be with her parents in Georgia after selling the farm to another young couple. The Johnston spread was still up for sale and the orphaned children were staying temporarily with the Rosses. The healing process of time was gradually alleviating the pain of grief and it was acknowledged that words would serve only to hinder this action of the passing days.

"Another?" Hayhurst asked, finishing his drink and watching as Edge sucked his own glass dry.

"Reckon not," the half-breed answered, smacking his lips in appreciation, then grimacing as he pushed himself away from the bar and glimpsed the overheated women near the piano. "Too much heat with too much beer and they might start to sprout wings."

"Aw, the *boys* are leaving!" Martha called derisively as Edge and Hayhurst headed for the batswing doors. "Goin' home to their mothers."

"Cut it out!" Jake snarled as he saw Edge's back stiffen.

"I might just as well, all the good it's doing me," the whore growled, running the sleeve of her dress across her sheened forehead.

The poker players laughed. "If you do, I'll have it, sweetheart," one of them called. "Make me a nice warm hat come winter."

36

"You sound like you already tried it for size," a second player drawled, leering.

"Jake!" Martha shrieked.

"Pack it in!" the bartender roared, knowing he was safe in venting his anger on the quartet of prospectors at the card table.

"Don't reckon there'd be any need," the leering man muttered, his voice not carrying beyond those seated at the table. "Figure there'd be room to spare."

Guffaws followed Edge and Hayhurst out on to the sidewalk. There was nobody else on the dusty street, the smell of woodsmoke laced with hot grease indicating that the citizens of Spearville were preparing for their midday meal.

"If you can wait awhile, I'll ride out to the lake with you," Hayhurst suggested. "My horse is down at the blacksmith's to be shod. Ought to be ready by now."

Edge nodded and took out the makings, watching Hayhurst's tall figure crossing the street and entering the stable beside the blacksmith's. He rolled the cigarette, lit it and allowed his eyes to rove absently over the façades of the sleepy buildings of Spearville, his mind idly recalling the many similar towns he had been in. On the surface, all had been much as this one, but beneath the surface there had always been one big difference—trouble. Either hiding there in wait for him, or following him in off the trail like an invisible shadow.

He was glad when Hayhurst re-emerged from the stable, leading a strong-looking mare, ready-saddled. For it cut across his reflections of a past he had chosen to forget. Hayhurst continued to lead his newly-shod horse across the street, but halted abruptly a few feet away from where Edge stood.

37

His stern features formed into a frown and he cocked his head to one side, listening. Then he shaded his eyes with a hand and stared out along the trail leading away from town to the east.

Edge had been so deeply engaged in his thoughts that he had failed to notice the sound. But now he heard it—the distant thunder of galloping hooves combined with the rumble of fast-turning wheels. It seemed to set the warm air trembling.

"Somebody's in one hell of a rush," Hayhurst commented as Edge gazed down the trail and saw the moving dust cloud drawing closer.

"Stage?"

Hayhurst shook his head. "Only Wednesday. Ain't due 'til Friday."

"Supposed to stop here anyway," Edge commented as the four horse team hauled their burden around the final bend and galloped along the town street without slackening speed.

Other people had heard the sounds of the hell-for-leather progress. Heads appeared at windows and doors banged open as Spearville's citizens sought to discover what was disturbing their midday peace and quiet.

It was now possible to see that the four horses, with bulging eyes and lathered backs, were dragging a covered wagon, flames licking at its frame, canvas flapping in the slipstream and wheel rims juddering over bumps and ruts.

"Ain't nobody driving it!" the fat Jake yelled.

"That's Ephraim Ross's rig!" Hayhurst roared.

Edge waited until the wagon had thundered in front of the saloon, then launched himself from the sidewalk into the saddle of Hayhurst's horse. Before the startled farmer realized what was happening, Edge had jerked the reins from his hands and turned the animal in a rearing wheel. Then the half-breed thudded his heels into the flanks of the snorting mare to send her galloping in pursuit of the runaway team and wagon.

The mare was fresh, with only the burden of a man on her back. She thrust forward her head and pumped her legs in a racing gallop that showed she was more than merely strong looking. She had been painfully spurred from a standing start with a gap of more than two hundred feet between her and the hurtling, smoking wagon. But the distance was reduced by half before the panicked team broke into open country at the far end of town.

The mare wanted to swerve to the side, so that she would not have to breathe in the choking dust through her flaring nostrils. But Edge, sloping his long body low alongside the neck of his mount, held her on a course directly behind the bucking rear of the wagon. He kept his mouth clamped tight against the dust and smoke, and cracked his eyes to slivers of blueness. The rush of air roared in his ears, drowning out the noise of the runaway and the drumming hooves of the horse under him. Then he was in the near vacuum immediately in the wake of the wagon and the clatter and crash of wheel rims and hooves sounded like an avalanche of crumbling rocks.

He urged the mare close enough so that he could have reached forward, and hooked his fingers over the top of the tailgate. Then he jerked on the reins, veering the animal to the side. Dust stung his face and clogged his nostrils. He flung his feet wide, kicking one free of the stirrup and crashed his heels into the flesh of the mare. She snorted in pain and lunged into what was almost a leap, carrying her half the length of the swaying wagon.

"Move it, you bitch!" Edge yelled in her flattened ear, stretching an arm forward.

The wagon team seemed to gain several feet as the straining horses swung into the right hand curve. But then the trail veered in the opposite direction. Through the billowing dust, Edge saw he was level with the charred high seat of the wagon. With the foot still in the stirrup and one hand on the saddlehorn, he thrust himself into a half crouch across the mare's back. As the tautness went out of the reins, the horse saw an opportunity to escape the agony of the blinding, throat-searing dust. She veered sharply away from the wagon's side.

Edge thrust himself aloft, kicking free of the second stirrup; bringing his other hand level with that curled to grip the rail at the side of the seat. His palms slapped the metal painfully and he clenched his fists. He brought up his knees and they crashed into the side of the wagon, ripping a groan of agony from his mouth. The ground raced beneath him in a blur. The offside front wheel spun within an inch of his right foot, threatening a crushing death if he should fall.

But he found a toe hold on the running board with his left foot, sucked in a deep, dust-heavy breath, and pushed himself up to the seat. His spine seemed to vibrate under the impact as he flung himself down. He spat vehemently into the slipstream and breathed in the clean air that rushed at him hotly across the backs of the straining team.

Then, abruptly, he saw the reason for the horses' panicked dash and he was ice cold in the intense heat. Tied to the rump of each horse was a muslin sack, the material woven loosely enough so that the angry hornets inside could not escape but could be

40

seen and could torture the crazed horses with their stings.

The reins were hitched loosely around the brake lever and Edge snatched them up and hauled on them. For stretched seconds, the pain-ravaged horses did not respond as every fiber in their bodies strained to escape the agonizing anger of the trapped hornets. But then, under the drag of the reins, the grab of the braked wheels and their own exhaustion, they slowed their hurtling pace.

They dropped from a gallop to a canter, then an ungainly trot. Edge prepared to launch himself forward, on to the back of the nearest horse. But, even as he streaked his hand towards the back of his neck, he remembered there was no razor pouch there. It was the last vestige of the old life he had shed. Two weeks ago, he had simply not bothered to loop the leather thong over his head before he dressed in the morning. And he had not missed the weapon—until now.

But, when the team finally came to a halt, they showed themselves totally drained of the will to escape their torment. Their hooves seemed rooted to the ground and the only movement was the heaving of their stomachs as they sucked in air to struggling lungs. As the dust settled, Edge jumped down from the seat and went to each horse in turn. He used brute strength to rip the buzzing sack of agony from the rear quarters of each horse, and tossed them to the ground in a pile. His heels stomped the demented hornets into silent extinction. The horses tried vainly to reach their punctured flesh with their teeth.

Edge had no preconceived notion of what he might find in the rear of the smoldering wagon. Hoofbeats sounded on the trail from town and a group of more than a score of horsemen galloped towards him as he unfastened the ties on the canvas flaps. He looked into the semi-darkness of the wagon and his lack of emotion at what he saw was a revelation of the lie he had been living over the past months. He had only seemed to become Josiah C. Hedges. Really, he was still the man called Edge— able to regard wanton violence and agonizing death with cold impassiveness.

The wagon's unwilling but now uncaring passengers were young Mildred Johnston and the dusky Mrs. Ross. They had been stripped naked and then pinned to the wagon bed with an arrow through the flesh of their inner upper arms. They had been scalped and their eyes had been gouged out. And that was not all.

The riders from town skidded their mounts to a dust-raising halt and stared into the wagon.

"And I made a joke about it," one of the poker players gasped, leaning to the side and emptying his stomach on to the ground.

Flies zoomed in to feed.

The hirsute triangles of the women's lower stomachs had been carved out of the flesh and hung atop two arrows which supported a strip of wood across the front section of the wagon. The women had spilled ample blood for the threat to be scrawled in red: stretching from one end of the board to the other—

WHITES ALL BIG ONES—SIOUX ARROWS SHAFT EM GOOD.

"Educate savages and all you get is dirty minds," fat Jake growled in disgust, spitting at the flies gorging on the heap of vomit.

The others in the group remained silent, staring at the blood-soaked bodies of the women, unable to speak through their horror.

"I need a horse," Edge said softly, turning to face the men.

"I need a drink," fat Jake responded, starting to back his horse out from the center of the group.

The horseman nearest to Edge had a rifle in his saddle boot. The half-breed slid out the weapon in a fast, smooth action. The man's gasp of surprise was lost in the metallic scraping as Edge pumped a shell into the breech. He aimed the gun at fat Jake, causing the big man to freeze.

"My need's greater than yours, feller," he said softly.

Fat Jake licked his lips nervously, recognizing the killer glint in Edge's eyes for the second time that day. "Men get hung for horse-stealing around here," he rasped.

"Around me, men get shot for not doing what I tell them," Edge replied. "Get down off the horse."

The obese bartender looked desperately around at his fellow citizens. "You goin' to let him get away with this?"

"Sioux are acting up again," Spearville's blacksmith pointed out mournfully. "This guy's wife is out here alone in the hills."

Fat Jake was not moved by the implication of this news. But the steadily pointing Winchester and the inaction of the men hurried him into climbing down from his horse.

"If that's acting, I'd hate to see what they do for real," he muttered.

"Obliged," Edge said, swinging up into the saddle of the bartender's horse. He looked towards the man whose gun he was holding. "I'm loaning the rifle, feller," he stated.

"You're welcome," the man replied.

The obese bartender ignored his knowledge of the

kind of man Edge was. He had been forced to back down at the saloon, and now for a second time, Edge had walked all over him. But he took out insurance by curling a hand around his holstered gun.

"Wouldn't like to loan one of my girls, would you?" he asked, a grin spreading across his fleshy face. "In case the Sioux creamed that farmer's wife of yours."

Fat Jake got the Colt clear of the holster, but there was not time to bring it up to the aim. Edge's expression altered only by the tightening of his mouth line. The Winchester had been resting easily across his knee. But suddenly, in the time it took the watchers to blink, he had angled up the barrel and squeezed the trigger.

The bartender screamed and dropped the revolver. His eyes were wide with horror as he watched the blood gush from his shattered wrist and cascade down his thick fingers.

"Not funny, Jake," Edge muttered, turning his horse towards town. "But for trying, you got a bloody big hand."

CHAPTER FIVE

Jake's horse was old and ill-used. But he made Spearville at a good gallop and responded well to Edge's insistence that he keep going instead of slowing for his usual stop outside the saloon. Jed Hayhurst, standing in front of a group of curious townspeople, shouted an inquiry to Edge, but the half-breed did not even try to hear what his neighbor demanded.

But the worried farmer realized Edge's haste meant the wagon had brought news of dire trouble. Edge had taken his horse and, angered by the half-breed's attitude, Hayhurst headed across the street to the parked buckboard with the cows tied on behind. Then, as he prepared to climb aboard, the first of the returning horsemen clattered into town.

"Indians killed two women!" the blacksmith yelled.

"The Sioux went us a warning," another man roared. "Looks like the uprising's getting started."

A tremor of terror ran through the waiting crowd and fear-filled eyes swept the street and strained to peer through the hills around the town. One moment the terrain was sleepily peaceful in the sunlight shafting through the haze. The next it was an alien world, brooding and menacing, filled with moving shadows behind which lurked a thousand kinds of vile painted death.

The dour Hayhurst was not susceptible to wild

imaginings. He knew only that Edge's haste was explained: that the half-breed feared for the safety of his wife. And Hayhurst found himself in the same position. The buckboard was not fast enough, but he was spared the necessity to take a horse by force.

"It was Mrs. Ross and the eldest Johnston girl," the blacksmith said as he slid from the saddle. "Take this nag, Jed. I'd come with you, but . . ."

The blacksmith was a widower with no children. He had nothing to protect except his own life but he could not bring himself to voice the conviction that he had a greater chance of survival in Spearville than out in open country. Hayhurst nodded to him curtly and mounted. He glanced around at the other men, astride their horses and standing in the street. All made a point of not meeting his gaze. A globule of saliva ejecting from his lips and spattering into the dust was a more vocal expression of his feelings for the men than any words he could have spoken. Then he heeled the horse forward, to race across the dust settled in the wake of Edge.

Far ahead on the trail, the half-breed knew the horse beneath him was tiring rapidly. But he demanded the limit from the animal, unmoved by the pain he was causing by stretching the straining piebald to the extent of endurance. Each foot covered on the trail curving between the hills formed a yard: and every yard mounted into a mile. And each mile that separated him from town was that much closer to Elizabeth. It was the logic of a fool, and Edge acknowledged this but offered the horse no respite. For he was equally aware that, when the animal finally dropped in its tracks, he was prepared to drive himself to the limit of his own stamina to reach his objective.

He heard the Indians before he saw them. Their

warcries carried shrilly across the lake, filled with sadistic joy.

"Come on, you bastard!" Edge roared at the horse, crashing his heels into the sweating flanks.

The animal struggled valiantly up the final rise, staggered over the crest and started to veer back and forth on the downgrade. Edge glimpsed the shimmering, dazzling expanse of lake water. Beyond, the cabin and new barn were still intact on the shore with the fields of ripening crops spread around. But the yard was filled with unsaddled Indian ponies, those which were unburdened by riders standing patiently still while those with braves on their backs reared and wheeled to the dictates of excited Sioux warriors.

In the instant before Edge's horse pulled up short and started to topple, he saw a group of war-painted and feathered braves burst from the cabin. And as he threw himself out of the saddle he received a blurred image of green and red at the center of the group. The dress he had bought for Elizabeth! He hit the ground with tremendous force and heard the much greater weight of the horse crash down beside him.

The Sioux had captured Elizabeth! The fact was seared into his mind with the burning intensity of a red hot branding iron. And then his torment was compounded by the knowledge that he could do nothing to help her. As when he had urged the horse towards exhaustion, he realized that his new act was futile. But the mixture of anger and anguish broiling in his brain nudged him to the brink of insanity. Every bone in his body seemed to be still vibrating from his fall as he snatched the Winchester from the saddle boot on the struggling horse. But the sight of the highly-colored dress among the joyful Indians excluded all else from his physical and mental awareness. He rolled over into a prone position and drew a bead on the dress. The braves were all mounted now, their cries of triumph reaching a crescendo as they turned their horses away from the cabin.

He squeezed the trigger and the crack of the rifle shot silenced the braves. The bullet made an insignificant water splash less than three-quarters of the way across the lake. Edge snarled and aimed high. The second bullet travelled a greater distance, but plopped harmlessly into the soft mud under the bank. The sound and futile result of this shot signaled a renewal of rejoicing among the Sioux braves, but this time their screams and yells had a derisive ring, taunting the lone white man.

The first brave burst clear of the yard and the others, raising their voices to a full-throated roar, streamed after him. Elizabeth's dress was like a flag of scorn among the vividly painted bodies. Edge gave vent to his own emotions, and a low growl rasped from his lips as he staggered to his feet and began to run down the slope towards the lake. He reeled from side to side on legs that seemed to have no bones or muscles. His right hand worked in a fluid motion, pumping the lever action and squeezing the trigger of the Winchester. The bullets set up a wild, crazy pattern across the surface of the lake and mud on the far shore. The Indians galloped away in triumph, riding in a wide curve that took them tramping across the wheat field and into the spruce forest behind the cabin.

The rifle ejected its last shell and Edge pulled up short, gasping for breath, his vision blurred by anger as he watched the stragglers disappear among the trees. Smoke curled from the kitchen chimney, rising lazily into the hot air. From this distance it was not possible to see the sign left by the unshod hooves of the Indian ponies and the spread looked peaceful and inviolate.

Then the sound of shod hooves caused Edge to whirl around. He snapped up the empty rifle and sighted along the barrel. Jed Hayhurst burst over the crest of the rise and started down the slope, casting a mere glance at the exhausted horse struggling to regain its legs.

He hauled hard on the reins, bringing his own mount to a skidding, snorting halt ten feet short of where Edge stood. The older man's stern face was pale beneath its weathered top surface. His eyes held Edge's demanding gaze with resolute steadiness.

"You chase them off?" he asked.

"From here I couldn't touch them," the half-breed replied. "But they got what they came for."

"Elizabeth?"

"Right. I need your horse, feller."

Hayhurst's expression did not flicker. "They already hit your place," he said. "Mine might be next."

Edge shook his head. "They went into the trees. Your spread's over to the south."

"So maybe they already been there," Hayhurst countered. "You want this horse, you'll have to kill me for it. I got a wife, too. And kids."

"Your problems I don't want to know about, Hayhurst," Edge said softly.

"Yours I can see for myself," Hayhurst replied. "A horse you run into a ground and a gun you emptied into the lake. I counted the shots."

He dug in his heels and the horse leapt forward, swinging around to the side of Edge. The half-breed lunged, swinging the rifle, but the wild blow went wide.

49

"Don't expect any help from town!" Hayhurst flung over his shoulder as he headed off on to the spur trail which led to his farm.

"I've learned to get along without help," Edge muttered, gazing scornfully up the slope to where fat Jake's horse had finally made it upright. "But I guess I forgot some of my lessons for awhile there."

As he hobbled up the hill, he became aware of the pain which attacked every part of his body, and of the intensity of the sun beating down out of cloudless sky. He talked softly to the dejected animal, coaxing him to stay still as he reached out and caught hold of the bridle. Then both man and beast moved slowly down to the shore and drank thirstily, the clear water warm in the shallowness of the lake's edge.

It was the only complete rest the half-breed allowed. For when both had drunk their fill, he gripped the bridle again and led the horse at an easy walk on a half circuit of the lake. When he reached the picket fence bounding the yard, he angled away from the waterside, keeping his eyes averted from the cabin. His own Winchester was inside, fully loaded and with a great many spare shells. So was his Colt, a Bowie knife and the razor. But his need of these weapons was negated by the knowledge that the cabin was also host to a thousand and one memories of happy times. And with Elizabeth, numbed by terror, in the hands of the painted savages—perhaps already suffering disgusting tortures or, mercifully dead—he wanted no part of what once had been. Later, maybe, when he had avenged her torment.

It was easy tracking across the fields to the forest, and easier still among the trees. In the shade of cool green foliage, both he and the horse recovered

50

quickly from their exertions. After an hour, when the animal's breathing had returned to a normal cadence and his eyes had become clear, Edge swung up into the saddle. The horse snorted a mild protest and tried a half-hearted buck. But Edge stressed his dominance, then made no attempt to drive the piebald faster than a steady trot. The horse settled into the pace contentedly.

The going was easy for the trees grew at adequately spaced intervals and the earth was for the most part free of tangled brush. The braves were moving at a fast rate and making no attempt to cover their tracks. When the signs showed the war party had swung to the south, in the direction of Jed Hayhurst's farm, Edge noted the fact without emotion.

The great forest cloaked a vast area of gently rolling ground but from the McCord place the bulk of it lay to the north and east. Edge had been traveling three hours, horse droppings giving an indication that he was closing with his quarry, when he reached the southern tree line. As he neared open country, the horse gave a whine of alarm and Edge reined the animal to a halt, eyes and ears straining for the first sign of danger.

The dappled sunlight was abruptly swept away, as if a dark cloud had moved into the sky. The horse snorted and Edge smelt the reason for the animal's nervousness: smoke. He dismounted and stalked forward, leading the horse. A shaft of sunlight pierced the billowing cloud of black smoke and dazzled him for a moment. He blinked and shaded his hooded eyes with a hand.

Jed Hayhurst's wheat fields were untouched, but in imminent danger of exploding into a raging series of fires as sparks from the blazing farmhouse drifted down on to them. Hayhurst was among the earliest settlers in the Dakota hills and had spent most of his waking hours building up his farm. He owned an entire valley, with better than two thousand acres of fine growing soil, naturally irrigated by a fast running stream with half a dozen tributaries. And at the center of all this had stood the once fine house— ten rooms and all of them furnished with loving care, each item constructed and fashioned by Jed and Bertha Hayhurst themselves. And every piece made of wood so that Jed could put his carving talent to use.

Now the fine house was fast becoming a blackened shell, the heat-shattered windows spewing out roaring flames and billowing smoke as the comfortable interior was consumed by the fire.

From his vantage point, at the top of a rocky escarpment overlooking the center of the valley, Edge could see Hayhurst standing before his life's work. The main stream which watered the fertile valley curved in close to the east wing, but Hayhurst made no attempt to douse the flames. He seemed like a statue, rooted to the spot. The blacksmith's horse was hitched to a gatepost, snorting and stamping in terror as it struggled to tear free and flee the flames.

"Obliged for your help, feller," Edge said to the horse he had taken from fat Jake. "You can go on home now."

He released the bridle and the animal wheeled abruptly and broke into a gallop, racing clear of the danger which smoke signified to its horse sense.

Edge, clutching the empty Winchester, climbed down the rocky cliff face, finding ample foot and hand holds in the weathered surface. Even before he reached the bottom, he felt the heat of the fire, which seemed to be held low within the valley by a sun determined to accept no challenge to its own burning intensity.

A new fire was already springing up among the wheat stalks in a field to the east and Edge broke into a run towards the solitary figure of Hayhurst. Soot and sparks whirled in thermals and were showered out to be wafted to the ground. They stung Edge's face and he smelled the dry odor of burned cloth as his shirt and pants became speckled with charred spots.

A freak air current kept the area in front of the house clear of fire detritus. But it did not protect it from the fierce heat of the flames. Edge shielded his face with his hands as he strode towards Hayhurst and halted beside him. The dour face, set in lines of depthless melancholy, was scorched in patches of bright red and snow white. Yellow heat blisters swelled on his forehead and jaw. He acknowledged Edge's presence with a quick glance, then returned his concentration to the house. Tears squeezed from his eyes and became vaporized in the heat.

"You could have had the horse," he said, and the words were as parched as the man himself.

"You see them?" Edge wanted to know, turning his back on the house as the ceiling of one of the rooms crashed in, exploding a fresh wave of scorched air.

"No, it was done when I got here. They butchered them all. Bertha, the kids. They cut the unborn child from her womb and defiled it. He was a boy."

"How'd you know, with this?" Edge asked, jerking a thumb over his shoulder towards the blazing house.

"Weren't them," Hayhurst muttered. "I burned the place. Didn't want anybody to see them after what the Sioux did to them." He looked at Edge now, for a long time, then asked. "Did you get any shells for that rifle?"

Edge shook his head.

Hayhurst nodded. "Have to be the way I planned it then."

He turned to face the house again, then started forward, holding his body ramrod stiff as the heat grew more intense.

"Hayhurst!" Edge called.

"You can't talk me out of it," Hayhurst answered, halting.

"Don't figure to," Edge told him. "Was a time I wouldn't give a damn about stealing from a dead man. But I'd like to have your permission to take the horse."

"Do whatever you like," the older man answered, and continued his walk towards death.

"Obliged," Edge acknowledged, and loped across to where the frightened horse was still struggling against its tether.

He spoke softly to the animal, quietening him, and stroked the scorched hair of his neck as he swung up into the saddle. He waited a moment before unhitching the reins, to look across at the house. Some of the kerosene which Hayhurst had poured around the rooms must have splashed on his clothing. For he was still more than six feet from the fiercely burning doorway when his shirt front exploded into flames. He screamed once, high and shrill, before bending at the knees and then leaping forward. His flaring body dropped short of the doorway and his fingers clawed at the dirt as he tried to haul himself inside. But death beat him and his body became motionless. The final shreds of burning clothing dropped from him and yellow heat blisters swelled up from the naked, roasted flesh.

"Didn't quite reach what he wanted," Edge said softly, making his voice a soothing whisper in the ear of the frightened animal. "But he sure got warm."

CHAPTER SIX

All the fields close to the house were raging seas of fire as Edge unhitched the horse and forced him into the swift-running stream. The animal fought against entering the water, but he plunged ahead gratefully when he realized that coolness combated the heat. Edge followed the stream in a north-east direction, veering his mount towards the center of the water-run as he passed between the blazing wheat-fields. Sparks stung and singed him again, and black smoke swept across his course like ugly night fog. The horse snorted and wanted to turn back, but Edge snarled at him and pounded his sides with his heels. The horse complied with the order to go forward, but elected to make his own pace. Water foamed and spray flew as the animal attempted to gallop through the stream which was fully three feet deep at the center.

Then animal and man burst clear of the smoke and swirling sparks. The green of trees on the valley sides and pasture on the lower slopes looked cool. The higher reaches of the stream had an icy sparkle. But this was all merely a trick of the imagination and Edge enjoyed only a few brief moments of comparative relief from the heat and discomfort. Then the afternoon sun reasserted that it had many hours of fierceness left to run. And, into his mind, seared the memory of the red and green dress standing out so starkly against the war-painted bodies of the Sioux raiders.

He had escaped the fire by the only route open to him. If he had been the kind of man who set any store by omens, he might have considered it lucky that the murder-crazed braves had left sign that they had fled the valley in the same direction. As Josiah C. Hedges, it was conceivable that he would have accepted this fact as an indication that fate was prepared to smile upon him. But as Edge, he merely saw the sign and followed it. It was simply there to be put to practical use. Had it not been, he would have circled the burning spread until he found it. An abstract factor such as luck played no part in his thinking: for it to be so, he would have had to have imagination. And a machine—which was what Edge became when the cold urge to kill possessed him—had no emotions. What he was, as he steered the horse up out of the stream and on a diagonal line towards the northern point of the valley, was little more than a series of reflex actions encased in a human form. The Sioux braves had taken his wife. Ergo he had to find them. They, or others of their kind, had murdered Jed Hayhurst's family and left tracks. Therefore, follow the tracks. When he found what he was seeking, he would have no weapon except an empty Winchester rifle. He had no idea what he would do then—for such a projection into the future required imagination.

When he reached the top of the valley side, he was confronted by the forest again. The tracks of the ponies—at least as many as he had seen leave his own farm—followed the treeline for half a mile, then turned into the timber at the rim of a narrow ravine which split through the forest like a gigantic knife

57

cut. It widened and deepened as he moved in the wake of the Sioux. Sunlight only reached a halfway point on the far wall as the afternoon grew old. The white water of a fast-flowing stream showed at the bottom and he could hear the roar and crash as water was forced between rocks. It looked cool down there.

Then the ground began to fall away in a gentle slope and he could see across a vast expanse of country. The sun had lost a great deal of its brightness and the approach of evening was sucking off the heat haze. To the east the forest appeared to go on for ever and to the north-west the rich green carpet extended to the long ridge of a high rise which limited the horizon. But due north, the timber began to thin, giving way to a barren tableland featured with rock outcrops and gently undulating sweeps of sun-browned grassland.

Wisps of smoke traced lazily moving patterns of grey against the azure background of the sky. Edge narrowed his eyes and pinpointed the campfire to the far side of a low butte in the middle distance. The clarity of the air played tricks with perspective, making it impossible to estimate how far it was to the camp—certainly more than twenty miles. The comparative freshness of the sign he was following indicated that the fire was not at a camp set up by the war party which had butchered the Hayhurst family.

The sight of the fire reminded Edge that he had not eaten since the breakfast prepared by Elizabeth before he left for town. But he discovered he was not hungry.

The horse seemed satisfied with the long, richly green grass he had chomped while Edge made his survey of the country ahead. And the animal responded willingly to the rider's demand for greater speed on the downgrade. First a trot, then a canter, until Edge called a halt at the bank of the stream. The Sioux raiders had also rested at this spot, to refresh themselves and their ponies with the cool water, which glided past smoothly here, before entering the rapids in the ravine.

Edge rolled a cigarette, and smoked it as he rode on, moving along the natural trail of a broad, grass-covered bank which sloped between the trees and the stream. The declivity and spongy texture of the earth suggested that the water rose to the timber line when the winter snows melted.

After a mile of straight running, the stream, narrowing with every yard, curved to the east and disappeared beneath thick growing brush. The Indians had left sign showing they had plunged into the trees and Edge went that way. He had been in the deep shade for less than fifteen minutes, his pace slow as the pony tracks became more difficult to see, when the twitter of a bird song took on a note of alarm, then abruptly ceased. Edge brought his mount to a silent halt and froze in the saddle, slitted eyes peering ahead and ears strained for the slightest scratch on the cone of stillness which had dropped over his immediate surroundings. Sweat held the leather reins tight against his palms. The horse's ears pricked and one forehoof raked the ground.

There was a *twang* of suddenly released tautness, a *swish* of disturbed air. The arrow streaked across Edge's vision and thudded into a tree trunk six feet to his left. Edge's eyes swivelled to peer into the timber on his right.

"You so much as think about reaching for that rifle, you're dead, mister."

It was a man, his voice scratchy with age and querulous with ill-humor. Edge turned towards the twig-snapping sound of his approach and regarded him with cold indifference as he emerged from the trees. He was tall and skinny, dressed in buck-skin pants and coon-skin hat: nothing else. In his bony hands he held a Sioux bow, ready slotted with an arrow and with the string drawn taut. The feathered ends of many more arrows showed above his left shoulder. His naked feet and upper body had a deep brown coloration from long exposure to sun. His face and utterly bald head were toned to an even darker brown, almost black. Age lines made his thin face ugly but his eyes—magnified enormously by the thick lenses of wire framed spectacles—were a paradox. They were black, with very white surrounds: clear and youthful looking. They sighted along the shaft of the arrow with steady intensity, promising deadly accuracy.

Edge guessed he was at least sixty and thought he could possibly be a decade older than that. "Don't let an empty gun worry you, feller," the half-breed replied softly.

The old man smacked his lips, showing toothless gums. "I got to be as old as I am by worrying about every little thing that didn't seem right," he croaked. "And a guy on his own in this forest don't seem right. Specially with the Sioux on the warpath. If that there Winchester really is empty, seems even wronger."

"You're on your own," Edge pointed out easily.

"I got used to me," the old man shot back. "What you want in these parts, mister?"

"Looking for a wife."

The old man didn't even blink. The arrow continued to be aimed at Edge's heart from a range of less

60

than ten feet. "Acting loco might make the Injuns leave you be, mister. But I'll kill you easier than spittin' you don't start talking sense."

"My wife," Edge went on in the same casual tone. "Raiding party of Sioux hit my farm and took her."

The old man made a sound of disgust deep in his throat. "Man wants to marry, ought to stay closer to civilization," he philosophized. "This ain't no country for women."

Edge had not moved since turning in the saddle to look towards the man. His muscles were beginning to ache from holding the same position for so long. But the unwavering aim of the arrow was a warning against trying to alleviate his discomfort.

"Obliged for the advice," the half-breed muttered. "Got any more?"

"Turn around and head back where you come from," came the reply. "If you find your missus, which ain't likely, you won't like what you see."

Edge shook his head. "Wrong kind, feller. Bunch of braves came through here awhile back, headed north. Where you reckon they're bound for?"

"Big war council up at—"

There was a scuttling among the brush and the old man swung around with lightning speed. He lowered the angle of the bow and released the string. The arrow took the jack rabbit in mid-leap, the needle-sharp point thudding into its neck and bursting through on the other side. Even before the animal's body hit the ground, the old man had jerked a fresh arrow from his back pouch and fitted it to the taut bow. But, as he whirled to cover Edge again, the half-breed was bringing the Winchester clear of the boot, pumping the action as he did so. Both men got their weapons into a killing position at the same

61

instant. The old man blinked now, and it was the only sign his confidence had been shaken.

"Force of habit. Never could resist the chance of a snap shot."

Edge curled back his lips in a cold grin. "Bad habit," he said. "Could get you killed."

The old man made the throaty sound again. "With an empty gun?"

"You believed that you wouldn't be just pointing that sticker at me, feller," Edge said. He kicked his left foot free of the stirrup and hoisted his leg over the horse's neck. Then his right foot came loose and he slid to the ground. The aim of the rifle did not leave the old man's heart. Likewise, the point of the arrow continued to be trained on Edge's chest, left of center.

"Ain't this what they call a stand-off?" the old man asked.

"I call it crazy," Edge replied. "I got no reason to kill you. And I reckon you aimed to hit the tree instead of me."

The old man considered the situation for long moments, then nodded and removed the arrow end from the string. He pushed the arrow back into the pouch, lowered the bow and thrust out his right hand.

"Name's Rubin," he said, stepping forward and showing his gums in the closest he could get to a smile. "Been trappin' in these woods for best part of thirty years."

Edge slanted the Winchester across his left shoulder and leaned forward, as if to accept the handshake. Instead, his hand swivelled into a palm upwards gesture, with fingers curled. He swung his arm and the old man gave a cry of alarm and staggered back. But not before the half-breed's fingers had curled under the eyeglasses and snatched them from the old man's head.

"Hell, I can't see hardly a thing without my glasses! he yelled, gazing myopically about him.

Edge tossed the spectacles to the side, so that they landed on a patch of soft grass and remained in one piece. As Rubin reached over his shoulder for an arrow, Edge yanked the bow from the bony hand. He thrust one end into the ground and leaned hard on the other. The wood was bent almost double before it snapped with a dry crack. Rubin's expression twisted, almost as if he felt a physical pain.

"You stinking, rotten bastard!" he hissed.

"The lying kind," Edge replied evenly.

Rubin's face showed anger. "Gun weren't loaded?"

"But I am," Edge told him, his voice hardening so that each word was spat out like a chip of jagged rock. "Chock full with hate." He reached out with his free hand and fastened a tight grip on Rubin's scrawny neck. "Most of it I'm saving up for the braves who took my wife. But I've got enough spare to spend a little on you."

"Jesus, what did I do?" Rubin croaked, his voice more rasping than ever now that it had to be forced from his constricted throat.

"You showed me the wrong end of an arrow," Edge snarled. "But people who don't know me get one chance to do something like that. If you ever get the drop on me again, kill me."

He tightened his grip and the old man was certain he was about to be throttled. He gasped and brought up his thin hands to try to wrench himself free. But before the almost fleshless fingers could fasten on Edge's wrist, the half-breed lifted him clear of the ground and flung him backwards. Rubin

63

hit the ground flat-footed, staggered and tumbled backwards. He sat down hard and cracked the back of his hairless head against a tree root.

"Real tough guy!" Rubin taunted. "Laying into a near-blind man more than twice your age."

"Easiest kind," Edge replied coldly. "Where's the war council, feller?"

"I only help friends," Rubin growled, rubbing his throat. "And one of them you ain't."

Edge sighed and side-stepped to where he had thrown the eyeglasses. "Not good at winning friends," he admitted. "But I sure can influence people."

Rubin was afflicted with acute short-sightedness. Without his eyeglasses he could see only colors and blurred shapes. His eyes bulged and his head craned forward as he followed Edge's movements. "I don't scare easy!" he snapped, but the tremor in his voice undermined the boast.

"That's okay," Edge told him easily. "We'll do it the hard way."

The half-breed looked around him, and saw a shaft of sunlight which pierced the foliage and struck the ground six feet from where Rubin was sitting. The old man yelled in alarm as one of his legs was grasped and he was dragged into the patch of sunlight. Edge plucked an arrow from the pouch and held the point hard against Rubin's throat, a fraction short of breaking the skin. Then he placed a knee on the narrow chest of his victim and thrust the eyeglasses into the bright shaft of sunlight.

Rubin was forced to remain inert on the ground, with the arrow point threatening death and the concentrated intensity of the sun's rays through the lens giving a warm promise of agony on the center of his forehead.

"Same burning question," Edge said softly.

Rubin gulped. His Adam's apple bobbed and the needle-sharp arrow point punctured his skin. Warm blood trickled from the tiny wound. Rubin's face was twisted by agony, but not from the cut. The unwavering dot of stark white light on his forehead exploded a searing pain inside his skull.

"The Peaks!" he shrieked.

Edge pulled the eyeglasses out of the sunlight. He could smell the charred flesh beneath the black spot on the brown skin. The arrow stayed within a fraction of bringing death to the old man.

"Far away, feller?"

"Thirty miles, north." Each word he spoke raised the lips of the small wound around the arrow point. Sometimes higher than others, to squeeze out fresh blood.

"Whole bunch of them going to be there?" Edge asked.

"Every brave in the territory old or young enough to fight," Rubin answered.

Edge nodded his satisfaction, then stood up. Rubin remained where he was, one hand massaging the burn on his head while the other fingered the wound at his throat. Edge crossed to pick up the coon-skin hat which had been thrown off when he first hurled Rubin to the ground. He returned to the old man and handed him back his property. Rubin saw him clearly again, and his eyes, enlarged to almost twice their size by the lenses, regarded the half-breed with a mixture of revulsion and fear.

"One more thing," Edge asked as he watched Rubin get on his feet.

"Yeah?"

65

"How come you know so much about what the Sioux have planned?"

Rubin stared hard at Edge, and now his magnified eyes showed only fear. For the half-breed's expression had become as hard as granite, with his slitted eyes glinting like precious gems through rock faults. The look was one of harsh suspicion, backed by the menace of swift and sure retribution if it was proved correct.

"Because I pay him to find out!"

The reply came from behind Edge and was punctuated by the dry clicks of a revolver as it was cocked. Birdsong had been absent for so long that the silence had been no warning this time. Rubin craned to peer around Edge's tall frame and he showed his gums in a wide grin.

"Howdy, Mr. Barker!" he yelled, with no attempt to conceal his relief.

"Drop it!" Rubin's rescuer demanded.

Edge let the Winchester fall. "It shouldn't happen to a dog," he muttered as he turned around.

CHAPTER SEVEN

"Heard voices so I held the boys back and came on ahead," Barker explained, eyeing Edge as if he considered him some strange specimen of tree but had no interest in natural history. "You want me to blast him?"

Barker was a well-built man of about thirty, with a two-day growth of gray beard sprouting from his jaw. But the hair on his head and that showing through his unbuttoned shirt front was jet black. He had easy good looks, overlayed with the negligent expression of the casual killer.

Edge readied himself to dive beneath the aim of the Colt clutched in the man's steady fist. But Rubin temporarily extracted the tension from the situation.

"Nah," the old man rasped. "He busted my bow and I reckon I deserve to give him what he's got comin'."

Barker shrugged. "Sure thing, doc. Okay if the boys bring up the wagon?"

Rubin chortled. "No offense, Mr. Barker, but it ain't been just you I was waiting for all week."

Barker displayed tobacco-stained teeth. He raised his voice to a shout. "Okay, bring it up here!"

There were a few moments of silence, during

which Rubin circled around Edge and went to stand beside the man with the gun. He looked at the half-breed with relish, like a hungry man anticipating a beef steak. Edge ignored both of them, turning his attention towards the sound of an approaching wagon.

It was a flatbed drawn by a two horse team, heavily laden and with the freight covered by securely lashed canvas. The driver had to take a zig-zagged route, picking out gaps in the trees wide enough to allow the wagon through. Two other men rode atop the concealed freight. When it stopped, all three leapt down, their hands hovering close to their guns as they looked curiously at Edge. They were younger than Barker. In their early twenties or even late teens. Each bore the same signs of long travel as the eldest man—embryo beards and crumpled, slept-in clothing.

"Trouble?" the man who had been driving the wagon asked.

"Nothin' I wouldn't have been able to handle myself," Rubin answered confidently, shooting a glance at Barker and receiving a wink of assurance that his secret was safe.

The trio of youngsters saw the blood on the old man's throat and the burn mark on his forehead. Then they looked at the unmarked Edge with the broken bow and Winchester at his feet. But none of them showed any interest in pursuing the matter.

"When will they get here?" the driver asked.

"Nightfall, I reckon," Rubin answered.

"You trust them for the money, doc?"

Rubin's chortling laughter was aimed directly at Edge and his enlarged eyes were brim full of joy.

"Raidin' party stole this here feller's wife. But I hear the braves have been hitting folks all over the territory. Reckon most of them finished the women on the spot and just took the money."

Edge marked down the anguish-raising taunt as one more score to settle with Rubin, and re-examined the bulky freight aboard the wagon. It was crated and there was no way to see the contents. But he guessed it was a load of guns and ammunition, with maybe some whiskey.

"So they got money," Barker said, a note of impatience creeping into his voice. "But will they hand it over or try to take the merchandise without paying the bill?"

Rubin rubbed his jaw reflectively. "I know a lot of Injuns better than I know any white man," he said. "And I wouldn't trust not one of them further than I can see without my eyeglasses."

Barker spat contemptuously. "That's just dandy," he growled. "I sunk my whole bankroll into this merchandise. Now you ain't sure you can swing a deal with the Sioux."

His impatience was swelling into anger, and he seemed about to concentrate it upon the old man. But his sense for danger prevented him from making the mistake and he kept his eyes and gun on Edge. The cold indifference of the half-breed was worrying him and contributing to his testiness.

"Hold on now!" Rubin said hurriedly. "I didn't say I couldn't swing the deal, Mr. Barker. Ain't you never dickered with a guy you didn't trust?" He looked at Barker for confirmation, but drew no response. The gunman, despite his advantage, seemed to be held in the power of Edge's steady, hooded-eyed gaze. "Course you have," Rubin went on. "So you know you have to take precautions. It's what I've done."

Barker jerked the gun forward. "There's a guy I don't trust," he growled. "Even though he's standing there without a hope in hell. If you want to do something about him do it now. Or I'll blast him for just looking at me like that."

The other three gunrunners looked at Barker strangely, then scrutinized Edge. And in his lean frame and inscrutable face they caught something of the aura of evil which had got to Barker.

Rubin shook his head emphatically. "Nah, Mr. Barker," he croaked. "I figured the plan I had in mind was pretty safe. But with this feller, we got us a seal on the bargain."

The driver cracked a personable grin. "Sounds kinda fishy to me," he muttered.

"He might carp about it," his blond-headed companion put in.

"Reckon not," the kid with a mole on his cheek supplemented. "Looks like a good-natured soul."

Barker thrust his left hip towards Rubin, offering him the holstered Colt. "You want him, you keep him on the hook," he instructed.

The old man hooked out the Colt and pointed it gleefully at Edge as Barker holstered his other gun. "Sure, Mr. Barker," he said with another chortle. "He won't get away from me." His eyes behind the thick lenses became vitriolic. "Ain't that right, big feller?"

Edge shrugged easily. "You got the rod, old man," he answered evenly. "And you can sure shoot a great line."

70

"Turn around and walk!" Rubin snarled.

Edge did so, but first threw a cold grin towards Barker. "Reckon he's scared I might blow the gaff?" he asked easily.

Rubin, with mounting anger, closed in behind Edge, but was careful to stay at better than arm's length from him.

"Where we going?" Barker wanted to know.

"Camped about a quarter of a mile from here," Rubin replied.

"Place we're going to meet with the Sioux?"

"Reckon they'll find us there," the old man told him.

Cursing, the driver climbed back on to the wagon and had to steer another crazy, corkscrewing course through the trees. Barker and the other two men, one of them leading Edge's horse, followed Rubin's path.

The old man had set up his camp at the side of a natural clearing in the forest. There were the ashes of a cooking fire, some dirty pots, a filthy bedroll and a sorry looking horse scattered on an area of level ground which would be shaded at midday. Now, late afternoon sunlight, robbed of intensity, sloped over the tops of the trees on the ridge to the west, casting long, individual shadows. The even ground stretched some forty feet from the trees bounding the south side of the clearing. Then it fell away in a gentle grade, about a hundred and fifty feet long and thirty feet wide.

"See?" Rubin announced excitedly after ordering Edge to halt. "My idea was to unhitch the team from the wagon and park it at the top of the slope. Then one of the braves would have come up with

71

the money. Soon as we got it we'd shove the wagon down to them."

Barker and his men regarded the surrounding timber with distaste. In the still bright light of afternoon the forest held no menace. But each of them knew that at night, even with a moon, they would not be able to see beyond the first ring of trees. The driver brought the wagon into the clearing and sensed that Barker was considering the situation. He spoke a final curse, wiped sweat from his forehead with his sleeve and waited in silence like the others.

"They could bring up five thousand braves and we wouldn't know about it," he said at length.

Some of Rubin's excitement drained away. "Hell, Mr. Barker," he complained. "We're dealin' with Sioux Injuns. You ain't never goin' to get no cast iron guarantees when you do that. You gotta take risks."

Barker spat, then jerked his head towards Edge. "Where does this joker fit in?"

Rubin's gums showed in a new grin as he met the cold, indifferent eyes of the lean half-breed. "For my first plan, one of us would have had to stay out in the open to dicker with the Injuns. But now we got us a front man."

"Lay it out, doc," Barker invited.

The old man did so, his scratchy voice tremulous as he enjoyed the pleasure of holding an audience. Barker responded to the plan with a nod, acquiescing without enthusiasm.

"Guess it'll have to do," he said, and glanced at Edge. "Hate to be in your boots, feller."

Edge shrugged. "Be too big for a punk like you."

Barker's expression darkened with anger and he

72

took a step towards Edge, hand curling around the butt of his Colt.

"Hey!" Rubin shouted a warning. "We gotta keep him in one piece."

Barker brought himself under control, and swung towards the expectant trio of youngsters. "Light the fire and fix some grub and coffee!" he rapped out. "Might be a long wait."

"It'll seem like a lifetime to him," Rubin said with a chortle, jerking the revolver in Edge's direction.

Aware of his importance to the gun-runners, Edge turned his back on the men and ambled over to the shady side of the trees behind the campsite. Rubin opened his toothless mouth to halt him, but realized his mistake in allowing the half-breed to overhear the plan. So all he could do was follow him. Edge ignored the old man and sat down, taking out the makings and rolling a cigarette. Rubin squatted down ten feet away and pointed the Colt.

While the driver relit the fire, the two other youngsters unloaded a sack of supplies and four Winchesters from behind the wagon seat. Barker stretched out in the shade under the wagon, the worried frown on his face revealing his lack of faith in Rubin's plan.

"Tell me something," Edge said casually when he had smoked half the cigarette in silence.

"Why do folks call me doc?" Rubin anticipated, the gummy grin splitting his face again.

Edge nodded. "Can't be because you fix up great operations. This one stinks."

Rubin's good humor expanded into a chortle. "Can't expect you to figure anythin' else," he allowed. "No, I'm called doc 'cause I end people's sufferin', feller. Lived in Injun land for a long time, so I've found more than enough folk dyin' slow deaths. I finish them off—quick like."

Edge saw the relish on the old man's face as his twisted mind recalled the countless tortured men he had killed.

As the meal was cooked and eaten—with Edge being offered nothing since Rubin maintained it was a waste to give food to a man due to die—the sun sank below the far side of the ridge. The light turned from yellow, through orange, into red. The moon appeared, almost full, as a pale white blob against the blueness of the sky. Then evening reached into night, as the gunrunners slept and Rubin continued his vigil over the prisoner.

There was no breeze to rustle the leaves of the surrounding trees. A crow winged overhead, croaking raucously, and settled on to its nest. Barker belched himself awake and blinked against the moonlight. An owl hooted, close at hand. Edge's horse stamped. The trees seemed to close in around the clearing, like an enveloping curtain of funereal black.

"Hey, doc!" Barker called.

"Yeah, it's time," Rubin replied, getting to his feet and gesturing for Edge to stand.

Barker rolled out from under the wagon and went to each of his men in turn, nudging them awake with the toe of his boot. Then, while Rubin continued to keep a close watch on Edge, Barker and his companions manhandled the wagon to the top of the slope, with its front wheels only an inch away from the start of the incline. This done, they picked up their rifles and moved off into the trees in back of the camp. Grunts and curses exploded from their lips as they climbed the gnarled trunks and settled into vantage points among the branches.

"You got him covered?" Rubin asked when stillness returned to the clearing.

"Like he was an apple in a barrel," Barker answered.

The others grunted to indicate that they had the half-breed in their rifle sights. Rubin pursed his lips in a silent whistle and thrust the Colt into the waistband of his pants. His eyeglasses gleamed dully in the blue-tinted moonlight.

"You know what you gotta do, feller?" the old man asked.

"Know what I'm going to do," Edge answered, curling back his lips in a cruel grin.

Anger made Rubin's face uglier than ever. "You got the choice, mister. Do like I told you and die easy. Cross me up and it'll be slow. And you'll have no reason to call me doc while I watch you die."

"Let's see which of us turns out to be the patient one, doc," Edge answered.

Rubin seemed about to issue another warning, but the snort of a horse far off in the trees halted him. "Get up there!" he hissed.

Edge fixed Rubin with a glinting stare, held it for a few moments, then hauled himself up on to the seat of the precariously parked buckboard. The old man gave a curt nod of satisfaction, then turned and loped off into the trees. When the sound of his climbing was done, the noise of the approaching Sioux Indians kept silence at bay.

Edge peered down the slope, conscious of the ri-

75

fles trained upon him: and of the equally clear target he would present to the Indians when they sighted him. He ignored Rubin's threat and the danger of the white men's rifles. If he should step out of line, they could not fire: because that was the plan—to let the Sioux take and torture him. He would only be shot, and thus die quickly, if he carried off the deal.

So the Indian braves—he counted eight of them, mounted on ponies—who had broken into the open and halted at the foot of the slope, were the immediate danger. They had white warpaint daubed on their faces, but wore no head feathers. Their clothing comprised fringed buckskin pants and sleeveless tunics fastened with thongs down the front. Two carried lances and the others had bows hooked over their shoulders.

Edge could see the whites of their eyes as they stared up the slope, picking out his form and the shape of the wagon against the less solid shadow of the trees in which the white men were concealed. He heard the murmur of the conversation as the braves discussed the situation. Although he could not understand a single word of the dialect, he detected a tone of apprehension in their soft chatter.

Then: "You got the guns for us?" one of the lancebearers called, speaking English with a guttural accent.

Edge remained silent and the seconds stretched.

"You hear me?" the Indian demanded.

Edge held his peace.

"Answer him!" A voice hissed from the trees and Edge recognized the speaker as Barker.

Some of the Indian ponies scratched at the

ground. The horses tethered at the campsite whinnied nervously. Edge raised a hand to his face, put a finger in his mouth and blew out his cheek. Then he bent back his wrist and the finger sprang out of the corner of his lips. The action produced a sharp *pop!*

"Ain't that clever?" he called, pitching his voice at a falsetto level. Then he emitted a cackle of laughter and sprang up into a half crouch on the running board.

"What's he doin'?" the blond-headed kid rasped.

Edge curled his fingers inside his shirt front and yanked downwards. Cloth ripped and buttons burst free. He threw himself up to his full height, expanded his bared chest and beat at his flesh with clenched fists.

"Howdy, Sioux!" he yelled. "Show us your muscles."

Down at the foot of the slope, the braves stared at each other, dumbfounded. Then, more nervous chatter erupted from the group. It swelled in volume as Edge continued with his antics, this time tearing at his long hair and screaming in apparent agony.

"He's gone crazy!" Barker hissed, glancing fearfully from the writhing figure of Edge to the confounded Indians.

"They say I'm loco!" Edge yelled, and began to pump his arms in imitation of steam pistons. *"Choo, choo, choo. Wooooooooooo-oo."*

"Bastard wants 'em to think that!" Rubin growled as the realization of Edge's plan hit him. "Injuns won't kill a crazy man. Figure he's got an evil spirit in him that'll haunt them."

Edge did not hear Rubin's verdict, but knew it would not take the old man—who had lived so many years in close proximity to Indians—long to spot the ploy. And there was no telling what he would do then.

"Stand clear! Stand clear!" he yelled. "Here comes the express. *Choo, choo, choo!*

"Woo-ooo-ooo-oooo!"

As he shrieked out the warning at the top of his voice, he began to jump up and down on the running board. For a seeming eternity, the buckboard remained stationary, as if imbedded in the ground. But then, with a series of creaks, the front wheels slithered to the lip of the incline. Edge jumped higher and thudded down harder. The front wheels rolled on to the slope. The buckboard canted and thrust downwards. The heavy crates of arms slid towards the front, adding impetus to the rolling free wheels.

"Ready or not, here I come!" Edge yelled. Then he flung himself down into a low crouch, fastening a grip on the hand rail of the seat as the buckboard juddered downhill, the speed increasing by the moment.

The braves were transfixed for several seconds, staring in horror at the buckboard hurtling towards them, out of control of the raving madman clinging to it. Then a rifle shot cracked against the creaking of strained wood and clatter of iron rims spinning over rocks.

It was Barker who fired, anger ousting confusion from his mind: an anger he was unable to contain as he saw several thousand dollars worth of guns and ammunition racing away from him. And directly towards the Indians who were supposed to pay him three times what the merchandise was worth.

But the Indians wanted no part of what was on the wagon. And it was terror of the crazy man, rather than fear of a crushing death, which broke through their own confusion and scattered them back into the trees.

Barker's bullet ricochetted off a wildly spinning wheel rim and zoomed high into the air. Rubin screamed for the men to hold their fire, but Barker pumped off another shot, and the three youngsters followed his example in ignoring the old man's plea.

Bullets smacked into the rear of the trundling buckboard, and then into the side as it veered off a straight course. Edge, his eyes slitted against the rush of air, saw the tense backs of the retreating Indians, then the dark curtain of the trees—deceptively soft looking. A stray bullet snagged at his tattered shirt and spurred him into making his move. He sucked in a deep breath, pushed himself up into a crouch, then leapt from the running board, lunging towards the upward slope of the ground.

He curled his long body into a tight ball, with knees tucked up to his stomach and hands clutched to his face, held low towards his chest. He hit grass with his left shoulder, rolled and smashed his feet into a tree root. A sound, like the breaking of every bone in his body, exploded in his head, heralding a searing agony that knifed through him from head to toe.

But he held on to his consciousness, and as his vision cleared he saw it was not his impact which had caused the noise. The buckboard had hit a jagged piece of rock and started to tip a moment before it smashed into the trees. Thus, as its forward momentum was abruptly halted, it began to roll over sideways. The ropes holding the covering in place snapped and the crates were hurled clear, smashing to the ground and bursting open. So that, as the buckboard rolled over and over to the foot of the slope, tearing itself to destruction, it left behind a trail of splintered wood, broken spokes, and spilled rifles and ammunition.

Shouts and rifle shots from the top of the slope left Edge no time to check himself for injuries. Summoning all his strength to fight a thousand and one areas of pain attacking him, he forced himself on to all fours, then threw himself into a half-standing position.

"Bastard!" Barker screamed down at him, backing the words with a shot.

The bullet, and three more, spurted dirt and wood chips close to Edge. Gritting his teeth against the agony, the half-breed forced himself into a staggering run. Gasps rattled from his throat as he stooped twice, one hand snatching up a brand new Winchester rifle and the other a box of shells—broken open but still better than half full.

Bullets whined about him, one of them grazing his shoulder. But the pain of this was like a mosquito bite compared with the bolts of agony being driven into his brain from the body-jarring fall. He reached the foot of the slope and threw himself into the cover of what remained of the buckboard, crazily tilted on its side. More bullets smashed into the wreck and he pressed himself against the ground. There was blood on the backs of his hands, oozing from deep grazes. But his instinct for self-preservation made his fingers work nimbly, pushing shells into the Winchester's loading gate.

The gunrunners kept up their rifle fire, crouched at the top of the slope and pumping lead at the overturned buckboard with the seeming intent of blasting it to tiny pieces.

Edge bided his time, knowing that anger and frustration were combining to blind the men to good sense: they were all firing at once so that only seconds would separate the emptying of one rifle from the others. And when this happened, he was ready. There was a final shot, then the click of firing pins prodding into vacant breeches. A series of curses ended the moment of silence which followed. Edge leapt to his feet and snapped the rifle to his shoulder. Five crouched figures were silhouetted along the top of the slope and he heard the gasps which signalled the men had seen him.

He squeezed the trigger and pumped the lever action as he swung to a second target. The first shot took the blond-headed kid through his top lip, blasted away his middle teeth and burrowed into the back of his mouth. Edge's next snap target happened to be Rubin, who turned to look at the dead kid at the moment the half-breed fired. The slug entered his side and was buried deep in his intestines. He was knocked on to his side and curled up his legs against the agony. But it didn't stop and he began to scream.

Barker and the others scampered back behind the cover of the incline's brow, fumbling fresh bullets into their rifles.

Edge launched himself out from behind the wreck and burst into the trees. Rubin's high-pitched screaming accompanied by Barker's string of curses, masked the slight sounds the half-breed made as he moved up the slope, just beyond the treeline. Then, when the trio had reloaded their rifles to capacity, they stretched out full length on the ground and bellied forward.

"Give it to the bastard good!" Barker hissed, and all three tilted the Winchester barrels over the top of the slope and sent a fusillade of shots towards the buckboard.

Edge reached the top of the slope to find them still engaged in this rage-motivated process. Their prone bodies were spread out for him like targets in a shooting gallery. The driver was the furthest away and the half-breed shot him first, killing him instantly with a shot that entered his head above the ear and tore a hole through his brain. Barker also died believing that Edge was still behind the buckboard. He took a bullet in the neck, which severed his jugular vein. The final kid saw the fountain of blood gush from Barker's throat and snapped his head around to look at Edge. He dropped the Winchester as if it had suddenly become red hot and rolled over on his back, thrusting his hands high into the air.

"Don't mister!" he implored, his voice silencing Rubin's screams and drawing the old man's attention to Edge.

The half-breed trained the rifle on the kid. One eye was closed. The other, behind the back sight, was narrowed to the width of a strand of spider's web, silvered by moonlight. The teeth, bared by curled lips in an evil grin, seemed not to be part of the burnished face that was their background.

The kid was the one with the mole on his cheek, who had made the crack about Edge being a good-natured soul. Now his wide eyes pleaded for the comment to have a slender thread of truth to it. His lower lip trembled and the front of his pants grew dark with a growing stain. He looked incredibly young and pathetically helpless.

"It's not true what they say," Edge muttered, and squeezed the trigger. The bullet went in under the kid's jaw, drilled a hole through his tongue and burrowed into his brain from below. His final breath sprayed droplets of blood, which spat back down on to his face like rusty rain. "Ain't just the good that die young." Then he looked into the magnified, pain-clouded eyes of Rubin. "But then you're living proof if it is so, ain't you?" he said.

"Finish me off, mister," Rubin begged, clutching his stomach tightly, so that more blood was squeezed from the hole in his naked side. "I deserve that much. I helped a lot of guys out of the spot I'm in." He gasped. "I could last for hours like this."

"Days, maybe," Edge suggested easily.

He began to move about the body-littered campsite, picking up the guns of the dead men and tossing them down the slope. The Colt revolver Barker had given to Rubin was the last to go. Then he turned free all the horses except the one he had taken from the blazing Hayhurst spread. He slapped the animals hard on the rump and they galloped fast into the forest. Rubin screwed his head around, watching the half-breed's actions with mounting fear.

"You just gonna leave me here to die?" he gasped as Edge swung up into the saddle.

"You figure yourself for some kind of doctor,"

the half-breed reminded him. "Know you're a sick man. Rest up for awhile."

"I'm dying, for Christsake!" Rubin groaned, pulling his bony knees in closer to his stomach. "Finish me off."

. Edge walked his horse across the campsite, checking that there were no weapons close at hand for Rubin to end his agony. When he was satisfied, he showed a cruel grin to the old man. "Reckon you'll live long enough."

"For what?"

"Those Sioux braves to decide the loco guy was killed in all that shooting and come back to get the guns they wanted."

Fear pushed pain from the enlarged eyes. "If they find me alive, they'll . . ." A fresh wave of pain curtailed the sentence.

"Bring you some bad medicine," Edge suggested, wheeling his horse away from the writhing form.

CHAPTER EIGHT

Edge rode south from the campsite, going back the way he had come. But he did not travel far through the almost pitch darkness of the forest; only to a point where the groans of pain and whimpers of fear from Rubin became a distant irritant against the stillness of the night. There, he dismounted, tethered his horse to a low branch and sat down to wait.

Just as every other facet of his life as a loner had returned to prepare him for the aim he had set himself, so did the capability of being able to sink into a shallow but nonetheless restful sleep. It was a sleep from which the slightest sound—even an intangible sense—of threatened danger would rouse him.

But when his eyes did snap open and every muscle in his body was galvanized into taut readiness, the signal was an ear-piercing scream. The sound quivered in the night and seemed to drive an icy blast through the summer warmth of the air.

The half-breed's expression was colder. He rose silently to his feet and gently caressed the neck of his horse, not unhitching him until the animal's nostrils had ceased to flare and the bulge had gone from his eyes. By the time even the memory of the agonized scream had faded into the distance behind the actual sound.

Edge led the animal by the bridle, retracing the path he had taken from the campsite. As he drew near, the silence of the forest retreated, backed away by the sounds the eight Sioux braves made in gathering up the scattered rifles and ammunition and loading them on their ponies. From his position, standing among the trees to one side of the clearing, Edge had a wide-angle view of the Indians' activity, for the moon splashed a gentle, silvered light across the open space.

The braves worked quickly and efficiently, and the expressions on their daubed faces told the reason for their haste. They were terrified! And the way in which their eyes raked across the surrounding black curtain of timber revealed the object of their fear— the crazy man, or the evil spirit which had been released if he were one of the dead.

They were halfway through their task when Edge first caught sight of them, and it took less than ten minutes for them to complete it. They left immediately, setting off at a fast trot as they led the heavily burdened ponies by the rope bridles.

Edge swung up into the saddle and urged his mount out into the open at the top of the slope. Rubin had got his wish that his agony should be ended. He must have drifted into unconsciousness for a while and come to his senses as the braves moved in around him, bows ready and aimed. They had recognized him as the man who had set up the deal, then double-crossed them. His eyes behind the spectacle lenses had been pulled wide by terror and his mouth had gaped to vent the awful scream. Three bow

86

strings had been released. Two arrows had shattered the lenses and sliced into his eyes. The third had thudded through the flesh at the back of his throat. His mouth was brimful of blood and two trails of red ran out of his eye sockets, with slivers of glass imbedded in them as the ghastly liquid congealed. The arrow which had entered his mouth had gone deeper than the others, penetrating through the back of his head and driving into the ground.

"When the Sioux make a point, they sure pin a man down," Edge said softly, and heeled his horse forward, heading him towards the gap in the trees through which the Indians had left the clearing.

The braves were making good time, confident that they had nothing to fear from white men or evil spirits once they were out of the clearing. So they sacrificed caution for speed and Edge was able to track them by sound instead of having to search the dark ground for sign. But this method placed him in danger of being heard by the Indians, and for this reason, he dismounted and tethered the horse lightly to a clump of brush as soon as he moved within earshot of his quarry.

As he loped away on foot, the animal watched him out of sight and then spent more than two minutes chomping at a patch of lush grass before pulling free of the brush. He wandered off in the opposite direction from Edge and the Indians.

The Sioux braves allowed themselves no respite on the northwards trek and maintained the gruelling pace. A hundred yards at their rear, Edge was forced to adopt the same tactic to stay in touch with them. Despite his height and weight, he could be extremely light on his feet when the situation demanded it, and the deadly game of tracking Indians from such short range made stealth of paramount importance.

Occasionally, a time-dried twig would snap beneath his boot or a low-hanging leafy bough would slap his face. But for the most part the sounds of his progress consisted only of the regular soft thudding of his running feet and the treasured rise and fall of his unlabored breathing. And such sounds were masked by the greater volume of noise created by the heavily-loaded ponies ahead.

Dawn came to the forest as a green tinted grayness, the light giving a false impression of coolness. But, as Edge slackened his pace, catching sight of the hindquarters of the last pony in the column, his face and bared chest through the torn shirt gave the lie to his notion. During the long night hours, the flow of air around his running body had kept his flesh cool. But now, as the new day underwent its birth pangs and the first rays of yellow sunlight penetrated the overhead screen of leaves, beads of sweat broke from his pores. The density of the trees grew less as the Indians and their pursuer neared the northern fringe of the forest. Edge had to breathe in more deeply to extract vaporized energy from the suddenly hot air: his shirt adhered to his back and salt sweat crystallized in his stubble and stung his eyes. It was not until full daylight struck him, swooping down upon the seemingly endless tract of waste land spread to the north of the forest, that he realized the extent of his weariness.

Ahead of him, away from the cover of the trees, the Sioux braves continued at their relentless pace, raising a cloud of dust from the eroded ground. But the nature of the life they led insured that they were always prepared for such a gruelling trial of strength. And, even as he halted, squatted and then stretched out full length in the shade of a tree, Edge had to admit to himself that he could not compete with the endurance of the Sioux.

Several months ago, before he began to share his life with Elizabeth, he could, perhaps, have stayed the course. But he had grown soft—was still harder than most other white men, but like warm butter compared with the flint-like quality of what he once had been. And the memory of old pains recalled the violent result of the leap from the hurling buckboard which had handicapped him from the start.

But his mind, ice cold with the determination to reap a terrible vengeance upon the savages who had stolen Elizabeth, refused to acknowledge physical exhaustion. He remained, spread-eagled on the ground, sucking in great gulps of dust-laden, over-heated air, for only half a minute. Then he folded into a sitting position and slitted his eyes to stare towards the northern horizon.

He saw that he was on the southern side of the desolate plain he had seen last afternoon. The terrain had more rises and depressions than it had appeared to have from the distant high ground, and the outcrops were larger and more grotesque from this angle. The column of Sioux braves and their ponies had gone from sight, but as he raked his eyes across the barren landscape, he saw them suddenly. They emerged on the side of a low rise, trotting up out of a dip. Neither man nor beast faltered or veered from the line set by the leaders and the pace was precisely what it had been at the start of the long run.

Edge lengthened the focus of his hooded eyes, tracing an arrow straight course directly ahead of the jogging Indians and ponies. What he saw made his lips curl back to show the twin rows of his even teeth in a grin. Yesterday, he had seen smoke rising from behind a low butte. From his new viewpoint, the butte was higher, and oddly shaped by a million years of wind and rain—curved in the middle with the rock sloping upwards to form a peak at each end, like a covered wagon with the canvas sagging between the forward and rear frame. More smoke trailed lazily against the azure blueness of the cloudless sky above.

"The Peaks!" Rubin had answered in response to Edge's question about the location of the Sioux war council. *"Thirty miles north."*

As the Indians went from sight again, this time the column curling around the foot of a pile of boulders, Edge rested his head back on the ground and closed his eyes. He estimated he had covered at least eight miles on the night run through the forest and judged the twin-peaked butte to be a little over twenty miles distant. It was a lot of ground to cover and one part of his mind urged him to get to his feet and continue with his pursuit of the Indians. But reason ruled impulse.

Despite the dim flicker of hope that Elizabeth might still be alive, the realist in Edge—and without Elizabeth he was entirely this—was convinced she was not. The Sioux were preparing for war and in the initial stages of this process they would allow

90

themselves an occasional diversion. But war to an Indian was closely bound up with religion and things spiritual. When the war council met and the chiefs made their inevitable decision there would be no distractions—and the pleasures of a white woman was in this category. And even if his wife still lived, Edge reasoned, he would be little use to her with the last ounce of strength drained from him—or a prisoner of the Sioux.

So he allowed himself to slip over the rim of awareness and into the refreshing softness of shallow sleep. It would build up his strength and allow the column of trotting Indians time to draw far in front of him, ruling out the possibility that they would see him when he set off in their wake. Now that he knew where they were going, they had served their purpose.

It was mid-morning when he awoke and, as always, was instantly aware of his present circumstances and his intention. The new day was as blazingly hot as the last. Nothing moved out on the uneven plain, except the shimmering mirages of sun-baked air. Even the smoke from the Sioux cooking fires seemed to be held like solid objects suspended above the heat-hazed shrouded butte.

Edge licked his lips and spat out the salt of crusted sweat. He felt dehydrated, but his stomach made no protest about its long lack of food. He jerked the brim of his low-crowned hat down over his forehead and levered himself to his feet with the Winchester. A bone in his leg creaked and every muscle in his body felt stiff and reluctant. But after he had strode out for five minutes, striking a direct line towards the stark landmark of the butte, he loosened up.

Fresh sweat began to pump from his pores the moment he moved into the full heat of the sun, reactivating the old. The musky odor of his own body rose to his nostrils. He attempted to combat the rancid discomfort by fixing in his mind an impression of the bitingly cold day of his wedding. Across this mental image there fell a vivid impression of the blood and entrails seeping from the ripped open belly of the Indian he had killed. The urge to see every Sioux brave emptying out his insides in such a manner set his feet on a quicker pace. But reason prevailed again and he forced his mind to become a blank, aware of the foolishness of overexerting himself in the harsh heat of midday.

From time to time, he saw signs of the Indians' passage. And when the tracks suddenly veered to one side, he knew the change of direction would not have been made on a whim. He followed the impressions of moccasined feet and unshod hooves, and suddenly broke into a run. A water hole shimmered like a patch of liquid silver. The Sioux and their ponies had almost emptied it, but there was an inch or so of water covering the bottom. The mud had settled from where the previous users had stirred it up and the water was crystal clear. It was warm and brackish as Edge stretched out full length and submerged his lips, sucking gently.

He stayed like that for a full two minutes, careful not to deluge his empty stomach with a sudden intake of the foul-tasting but life-sustaining water.

"We gonna die you, white woman."

Edge became as unmoving as a block of carved

92

stone. He had almost emptied the hole of water. But as he ceased sucking, the ripples settled and there was just a deep enough covering of the mud to form a mirror. Two Sioux braves stood on the far side of the hole, about six feet away. They were naked except for heavily stained gold-striped cavalrymen's pants. Each held an ancient Spencer rifle and when Edge slowly raised his head a muzzle was directly in line with each of his eyes.

"Your English ain't good, but it's better than my Sioux," the half-breed said softly.

They were both young—sixteen or seventeen—and wore no paint and just a single feather at the back of their heads. Edge's hooded eyes looked beyond them, seeking out their ponies. But the animals were concealed, possibly in amongst a strange rock formation that looked like a clump of petrified trees with the branches lopped off. He guessed the youngsters had been out hunting for food, interrupting the work to take a drink.

The second brave erupted a burst of rapid chatter in his native tongue. His companion craned forward to peer into the water hole. Edge's left hand curled around the brass frame of the Winchester which lay at his side.

"My sister happy you eat all water," the one who thought he knew English spat angrily.

Edge moved the Winchester forward an inch, so that his fingers could curl through the lever grip. He showed the Indians his cold grin.

"Lot left if she's wet," he said, matching the crazy, opposite idiom of the spokesman.

He guessed the kids had not yet killed a man. Had they been fully-fledged braves, they would have undoubtedly blasted him on sight. But even now, as the half-breed tightened his grip on the rifle and tensed his body to prepare for a roll, they exchanged more of the guttural sounds which were intelligible to each other. Edge guessed they were discussing whether they would earn greater honor by simply killing him, or making him a captive and taking him back to camp. The apprehensive glances they shot in Edge's direction suggested that neither alternative was wholly appealing.

Finally, the spokesman nodded his head in emphatic agreement and tried to appear tough as he regarded the white man. "You gotta be died, white woman," he rasped. His eyes gave a good impression of hardness, but his lips took on a tremor he could not control. "I first born so my sister die you."

He meant his brother was the oldest, so he was to get the honor of shooting Edge. He turned towards his brother and gave a nod. Edge rolled. He went to the right, flinging himself hard on to his back. His right hand came free of his moving body and steadied the Winchester as his left pumped the action and squeezed the trigger.

The Spencer roared a half second after the crack of Edge's rifle. But the bullet whined across the barren terrain on a decaying trajectory. For when he squeezed the trigger, the young Indian was already falling, the rifle pointing skywards. The bullet from the Winchester had punctured a bloody hole in his right cheek and burrowed through his brain to exit from his shattered skull.

Edge had fired the shot from an upside-down position. Now he continued the roll, coming to rest with his body prone as he aimed at the second Indian. But this kid was no threat. He had dropped the Spencer and fallen to his knees beside the still form of his brother. He stooped low and embraced the dead head with its gruesome outpourings of blood and sticky gore.

The half-breed got to his feet, maintaining his aim at the grieving Sioux. The boy turned a tear-run face towards him. "You died her!" he accused.

"Still looks like a red Indian to me," Edge said softly. "You're the blue one—and that ain't natural."

The Winchester spat death a second time. It was another head shot, entering the forehead. The hole made by the bullet was neat. The blood it spewed was messy. Red Indians were never that color until blood ran across their brown skins. This one had a surfeit of it and spared some to spray over his brother as he toppled sideways into the dust.

Edge dug two fresh shells from his pants pocket and pushed them through the Winchester's gate as he moved around the water hole. Then he used the stock of the rifle to push the heads of the youngsters up close, one to the other. Blood seeping from the forehead wound met that coating the cheek. It was even too hot for flies to be on the wing and the blood congealed without hinderance, linking the two dead Indians.

"Brothers ought to stick together," Edge said vehemently, and spat on the rapidly drying bond. Then he went to look for the boys' ponies.

CHAPTER NINE

The Indian youngsters had been no better at killing animals than a man. They had shot a jack rabbit and a young deer which was a poor hunt over so many miles. The raw meat had no appeal even to Edge's empty stomach and he did not want to take the time to make a fire, prepare one of the animals and cook it. But he did not untie the rabbit from around the neck of the pony he chose to ride, deciding that as the second day without food progressed, he might be forced to waste time with eating.

The Sioux pony was small but strong. It was a sorrel stallion and he bore the heavy weight of his new rider without complaint. Getting to understand and carry out the commands of Edge was a greater strain on the pony, but eventually the magic rapport that an experienced horse rider can generate between himself and his mount came about.

After allowing the pony to suck up what was left of the water in the hole, the half-breed started out towards the twin-peaked butte. The sky stayed big, blue and clear throughout the afternoon: its only blemishes being the wispy woodsmoke of Sioux fires. The sun burned down and no relief was offered against its fierce heat until the shadow of the lone rider was a very long splash of darkness pointing to the east.

He did not push the animal hard through the furnace of the day, but when evening beckoned with a softer light and cooler air, he urged the sorrel into an easy canter. His objective was much closer now, and much bigger in perspective. He could pick out detail and color. The peaks at each end towered to about six hundred feet and dropped almost sheer on their outer faces. But the ridge which linked them sloped much more gently, curving down to a low point of some three hundred feet above the level of the surrounding terrain. The entire uneven block of black, gray and white rock streaked with red was silhouetted against the northern skyline for more than two miles.

The old, but occasionally still visible tracks left by the party of Indians, led towards a midway point in the butte. This fact caused Edge to halt his pony when he was a little over a mile from where the rock reared up from the floor of the barren wasteland. The back of his hand made a rasping sound as he rubbed it over his stubbled jaw. His tongue tasted salt sweat as he moistened his lips. His eyes, which had been narrowed against the harshness of bright sunlight for so long, now became mere slits as they examined the vista ahead of him.

There was no well-trodden pathway up to the lowest point on the ridge and he picked out a dozen ways to the top. But every one of these was wide open to the danger of ambush. For the dying sun, spraying in low-angled, pink-tinged light from the west picked out countless shadowed places where watching braves could be lurking. And if the Sioux

97

had posted sentries to guard the southern approach to their camp, the waiting braves would be able to follow Edge's progress up to the ridge for almost every foot of the way.

The alternative was to move in close to the start of the rise and then circle around the foot of the butte.

He spent only seconds considering the choice, then signalled his decision by sending a globule of saline saliva into the dust. If there was just one Sioux brave crouched in a shadowed pocket of rock on the butte, he would have had Edge in sight for the past two hours or more.

"Reckon we'll go over the top, feller," he said to the pony and heeled the animal forward.

But only to the point where the rise began. There, he halted and dismounted. He looked for and found a cleft in the rock where he could rest and wait out the evening and not be seen from above. Hunger began to gnaw at his stomach now and he untied the jack rabbit from around the pony's neck. The large gunshot hole in the animal's head had turned rancid in the heat. The body meat would still be good, but Edge suddenly flung the limp body out of his hiding place, cursing himself for a fool.

He had no means of skinning and cleaning the rabbit. There flashed across his mind an image of the two dead Indian boys back at the water hole—he even saw the knife hilt protruding from the waistband of their pants.

He acknowledged his failure to take one of the knives as a sign that he was not yet the man he once had been. He could still kill as mercilessly as ever, suffer pain and endure privation with the same degree of unrelenting purpose that had strengthened his character before his marriage. But his brain had failed to re-adapt itself at the same rate as his bodily reflexes. The need to achieve was a more powerful force than reasoning the means to the end and Edge knew that, in the task he had set himself, such a situation would inevitably lead to failure.

So it was that, as he sat in the rock cleft under a darkening sky, he forced himself to shed the last vestiges of Josiah C. Hedges. He thought he had achieved this before, but anger and grief had colored his thinking. It had been at its strongest when he had shunned entering the cabin to get his weapons. Time and the miles on the trail of the Indians had seemed to weaken the influences of the twin emotions which the man called Edge would never have allowed himself to feel.

Elizabeth was dead, killed by a band of Sioux raiders. To avenge her death would require detailed planning and cold-blooded execution of the resultant scheme. Only a fool would set out to kill with his mind loaded with anger. Josiah C. Hedges had been a fool a long time ago, when he tracked down the killers of his brother: driven on by white hot fury from Iowa to the Mexican border. He had been lucky. Now he had been a fool for a second time and luck had been with him again.

Edge got to his feet and stared with hooded eyes up the moonlit slope of the rock barrier between himself and the Sioux. Hedges had about used up all the luck any man was entitled to expect. Edge didn't need it!

Moonlight had toned down and merged the colors of the rock formation to an all-over gray, except where knolls and depressions provided patches of menacing darkness. The half-breed's eyes raked over the rise time and time again, alert for the slightest sign of danger. But there was none. It meant nothing. He knew the Sioux of old, when he had fought as a boy alongside his parents and brother to defend the family farm from their raids. And in more recent times he had tangled with the Apaches and Shoshonis.* But whatever their tribe, all Indians shared an inbred patience, cunning and stealth. Thus, Edge realized there could be one or a hundred-and-one braves peering down at him, content to wait for him to make the first move.

He made it—slapping the pony hard on the rump. The sorrel gave a snort of protest and lunged forward, galloping along the foot of the rise and then suddenly swerving and heading up the slope. His hoofbeats were very loud against the stillness of the night.

Edge went in the opposite direction, dropping into a crouch and running. He ducked into another cleft, but this one had a sloping floor which gave access to a way to the ridge. He came out of it and halted behind a jagged protection of rock. His eyes made another minute surveillance of the slope. The pony was slowing on the steepening upgrade, but he knew where he was going and did not hesitate before making any move to left or right. He was following a course he obviously knew from habit. Nothing else moved on the slope.

Edge darted from cover, the Winchester levelled from the hip. A boulder was balanced on a ledge up

*See—Edge: *Apache Death* & *Edge: Blood in Silver*.

and to his right. Loose pebbles rolled from beneath his boots and sounded like an avalanche. He halted, looked and saw nothing. The night seemed to grow hotter. Sweat stung his eyes and he wiped it away with the back of his hand.

A whistle cut across the diminishing sound of the galloping pony. The sorrel reached the ridge and disappeared from sight. Edge recalled the piercing sound of the Sioux signal a moment before the two braves exploded death on his wedding day. The Indians *had* posted sentries on the south face of the butte. They had seen him riding towards them through the late afternoon and had waited patiently for him to emerge from the cleft.

As he crouched behind the boulder, more pebbles rolled, but these were disturbed by moccasined feet. The sound came from the right, at least forty or fifty yards away. But in that general direction there were at least a dozen dark hiding places. The whistle had come from directly ahead, close to the top of the ridge. Nothing moved up there.

Edge tensed himself, readied the rifle for snap shooting and lunged out of his cover. He didn't see the lance arcing up into the air. But he heard its hissing approach from the dark and flung himself into a rolling dive. The lance powered into the rock less than three inches from his leg, spitting tiny fragments. A brave dropped down towards him from an overhang, knife raised at the start of a swinging thrust. His painted face was twisted by a grin of triumph. Edge was on his back, with the barrel of the Winchester momentarily trapped under his thighs. He released his grip on the weapon and threw himself into another roll, which brought him down lengthwise on the lance.

The brave could not adjust his direction in mid-air and thudded to the ground in the space vacated by Edge. He landed on his feet and immediately spun around, the knife slashing. Edge raised himself on to his haunches then, fluidly, into a crouch. The brave grunted as his first slash skimmed over the half-breed's head. The knife was turned by a flick of his wrist and started on a back-hand, stabbing thrust. But Edge threw himself upright, bringing up the lance in a powerful drive. The brave's naked belly was sucked in as he tensed for the killing knife thrust. The point of the lance burst into his flesh like a needle entering the skin of a rotten apple. The brave's scream, as he dropped the knife and clutched at the shaft of the lance, seemed to fill the entire world with high-pitched sound destined to continue for eternity. His eyes expanded to monstrous proportions.

Edge grinned coldly into his pain-twisted face and drove the lance in deeper. Blood erupted from around the shaft and sprayed over the brave's hands. Death came to him and Edge let go of the lance, allowing the Indian to crumple to the ground, still gripping the smooth wood.

"Bad way to check out," the half-breed hissed, scooping up his rifle and the brave's knife. "Should have stayed with the reservation."

He glanced around, finding himself in the open. Another lance arced towards him and he flattened himself against the overhang. The metal tip of the lance glanced off the rock face and slithered down the slope. A shape loomed up among the shadows above him and moonlight glinted on metal. He flung the rifle upwards and squeezed the trigger. The stock recoiled viciously against the top of his shoulder. The death scream of the brave masked his own groan of pain. The body thudded to his feet and emptied blood from a punctured heart.

One glance was enough to see that the Indian was dead and Edge pivoted and peered up the slope as pebbles rattled. He saw movement and pumped the Winchester's action as he brought the rifle around to the aim. He fired. The bullet took the running man in the hip. He pulled up short and started to turn, fighting to save himself from falling. But shattered bone gave up the struggle and he toppled. He fell over the lip of a ledge and slithered down headfirst, his arms stretched out in front of him. Edge stepped into his path, the knife poised. He rocked back on his heels, then forward, flat-footed. His boots came down hard on the brave's hands, trapping them. The brave twisted his body, then kicked upwards with his good leg.

Edge swayed to the side, then swung his arm. The knife slashed through the brave's flesh and severed his achilles tendon, pouring blood on to his own face as the leg fell away.

"You ain't very sweet Sioux," Edge rasped. "Fact is, you're a bad heel."

He stooped and the brave screamed. The sound became a gurgle as the knife plunged into his throat.

"But now you're a good Indian," he said, straightening up.

He was in time to see another brave, running full tilt, reach the crest of the ridge. He let the knife fall back on to the dead body at his feet and snapped up the rifle to his shoulder. He squeezed the trigger at the moment the full height of the brave was silhouetted against the skyline. The Indian was halted in his tracks, frozen there for a moment, then crumpled. The bullet had shattered his spine and he was transfixed on the crest of the ridge, completely paralyzed.

Edge was not an expert on the lore of the Sioux. But he knew that a brave of that tribe would never run unless the odds were stacked high against him. One white man with a rifle against one Indian with only a knife, or maybe a tomahawk, added up to the brave being a loser.

So, confident he had killed every guard on this side of the butte, Edge started up the slope. He walked erect and whatever cover he had was gained simply because the terrain presented it in his path. But his eyes and ears were alert for the first sign of danger, and the rifle was held in a diagonal line across the front of his body, ready to swing to the aim at an instant's notice.

But, when a target presented itself, it was just one of at least two hundred. They had advanced up the north side of the butte in a curved line, drawn by the sound of the rifle shots. Thus, every war-painted brave appeared on the ridge at precisely the same moment.

Edge halted, and swung the Winchester to his shoulder. He aimed for the heavily-feathered subchief at the center of the line, then raked the sight to left and right. Two hundred rifles, supplied by Barker and others like him, returned Edge's steady aim. The sub-chief was the only man in the unmoving line who did not carry a rifle. Instead, he held a highly-decorated lance. The paralyzed brave on the ground in front of him grunted his agony.

"He run away from you?" the sub-chief demanded of Edge in a guttural tone.

The half-breed settled his aim on the red, blue and white paint striping the spokesman's chest. "He tried."

The lance rose slowly, then drove downwards. The paralyzed brave died with a gasp. The sub-chief crouched, drawing a knife. The blade sank deep into the dead flesh, then spurted blood as it sawed in a circle around the bloodied shaft of the lance. The braves continued to train their rifles on Edge. The sub-chief stood up, worked the lance in a circular motion, pushed it to one side and jerked. There was a moist, sucking sound.

He thrust the lance high in the air, staring with cruel eyes at the prize spiked on the point. Blood oozed from the pulpy chunk of flesh and the ripped-out heart. It trickled down the loose hanging tendrils of broken veins and arteries to drip to the ground.

"You see how we treat Sioux cowards?" the sub-chief taunted Edge, unafraid of the half-breed's pointing Winchester.

"You must have a lot of heart," Edge answered sourly.

"Pretty damn funny," the educated Indian shot back, whirled the lance and tilted it. The gristly human meat and heart arched through the air and splatted against the ground only inches in front of Edge. Droplets of blood splashed on to his dusty boots. "You don't drop that rifle by the time I reach zero, you'll be pretty damn dead."

105

He started to count, beginning at ten and working backwards. Edge continued to train the Winchester on him, raising the aim to the handsome, self-assured face. He saw only the sub-chief, but was aware of every other brave and the unwavering rifles in their hands.

". . . seven . . . six . . . five . . . four . . ."

Edge sighed and released his grip on the rifle. It clattered to the ground. "Okay, hold," he muttered.

The sub-chief grinned. "You don't want to get blasted, uh?"

"Ain't exactly over the moon about it," Edge growled.

CHAPTER TEN

The stories had been right. The Sioux were massing and there could be only one reason for the vista spread before Edge as he complied with an order from the sub-chief and moved up to the crest of the ridge. To the north of the butte there was an enormous depression in the barren land in the shape of an almost perfectly circular crater. Erected in neat rings, spiralling to the center, were something close to a thousand teepees. The encampment showed up clearly in moonlight which was supplemented by the wavering glow of hundreds of cooking fires. To one side of the camp, corralled here by a dry-stone wall erected by the braves, were a couple of thousand head of ponies. Edge had no doubt that the braves he could see moving among the teepees or sitting by the fires were daubed in similar fashion to those who had captured him. A gathering on such a scale had to mean the Sioux were on the brink of an uprising.

He sensed the eyes of the sub-chief on him and looked towards the garishly-painted face. The grin was still broad and bright, almost charming. In this mood he looked incapable of even thinking about cutting out a man's heart.

"How about that?" he asked proudly, waving a

hand to encompass the enormous camp. "This what you were scouting for?"

Edge rolled saliva around in his mouth and spat it out in a stream. "I was prepared for it," he answered.

The sub-chief jerked his head and Edge complied with the signal to start down towards the camp. The slope was gentler on this side and less broken, leading into the gigantic depression over which the teepees were spread. The good-looking young sub-chief walked slightly behind him, covering him with his own Winchester. Six braves toted the three guards who had fought bravely and died badly. The others formed into a three file column behind Edge and the sub-chief.

Whatever the braves and squaws had been doing previously, they all considered their tasks unimportant enough to let them wait. Because of the symmetrical way in which the teepees had been positioned, it was possible to enter between any two in the outer ring and have an unobstructed path to the open area at the center.

The curious bystanders, converging from every section of the camp, formed themselves into silent, orderly rows which clearly marked out the way Edge was expected to take. The lack of sound from so many watchers had an eerie quality, accentuated by the menace emanating from the hundreds of staring, brooding eyes.

As Edge strolled casually between the watchers, his own eyes swung to left and right, replying to their hate with a cold indifference.

"I don't appear to be very welcome," he tossed over his shoulder to the grinning sub-chief.

"You killed three of our braves," came the guttural reply.

Edge raked his eyes over the crowd again. "Plenty more where they came from," he pointed out.

"It's good you regard life as so cheap. Yours ain't worth a cent."

"Didn't they teach you not to say ain't in that school you went to, feller?" Edge asked as he emerged into the open, central area of the camp, the focal point of which was a twenty foot high totem pole.

"I'm learning to forget everything I was taught in that place," came the reply. "Halt!"

There was a sudden disturbance in the crowd, which had been breaking up out of the two lines to form a circle around the open area. This had proceeded as quietly as the crowd had at first formed, but a shout followed by a burst of rapid fire Siouan signalled a general hubbub of excited conversation. Edge looked at the brave who had started the disturbance and found the man pointing at him with a trembling finger.

The half-breed glanced at the sub-chief.

"He says you're a mad man," the Indian explained. "Got an evil spirit in you. He thought you'd been killed over in the forest."

Edge shrugged. "Maybe I was. Maybe I'm a ghost."

The sub-chief brightened his grin. "One of the things I won't forget I learned. Indian superstition is as much crap as the white man's black cat and rabbit's foot."

"Don't scare you, uh?" Edge asked.

The sub-chief moved around in front of Edge and met the half-breed's level gaze. Deep in his own eyes, as brown as Edge's were blue, was a message that he understood the kind of man he had captured. "Not while I've got this Winchester aimed at you," he said simply.

Abruptly, the disturbance was over. There was no trailing off of noise, with nudges and whispers. Just a sudden cessation—sound then silence. The crack of logs on the many fires even seemed halted for several moments.

"Turn to face Chief Black Hawk," the sub-chief commanded. Neither his tone nor his expression held the slightest degree of good humor now and his veneration for the chief showed as strongly as it did in the faces of the braves and squaws of lower status.

Edge swung around casually and regarded the imposing Indian who had stepped through the flap of a teepee much larger than all the others in the camp.

Black Hawk was tall for a Sioux—almost six feet. He was about thirty-five and had a smooth handsomeness beneath the daubing of warpaint. His build was broad and muscular, the flesh rippling with latent strength as he straightened from a stoop and took two steps forward before halting. He wore a buffalo hide robe decorated with quills, a skin shirt and leggings tied with thongs. His heavily feathered headdress reached to his ankles. As he placed his arms akimbo and surveyed Edge with a dark stare from his jet black eyes, the half-breed sensed the ambiance of power emanating from his intelligent face and strong body.

"What he here for?" he demanded of the sub-chief. "I say all pale faces kill quick."

110

The sub-chief replied in his native Siouan and spoke for a long time. The way he held up three fingers and the look of surprise and then hate which showed on Black Hawk's face suggested to Edge that the story of his assault on the south side of the butte was being told.

Edge held the chief's gaze for long moments, and it was Black Hawk who finally submitted, a grimace revealing his feelings about it. Then, as bursts of Siouan were exchanged between the big chief and the sub-chief, he glanced around at the watchers. His attitude was arrogantly casual, but then he spotted something that caused him to fix his gaze and tense his body. The braves were dressed in a great variety of clothing, some of native make and some stolen from the army and white civilians. One of them, whose attention was captured by Black Hawk to the exclusion of all else, was wearing the bodice section cut from Elizabeth's red and green dress.

The half-breed held himself in check, fighting back the rage which threatened to explode from his mind and trigger physical action. Many of the braves carried rifles and all would have a knife or tomahawk. And despite the near reverence of their whole-hearted attention to Black Hawk, Edge knew he would not be able to get within ten feet of the brave he wanted before death struck at him from every direction. So he just stood and looked, fixing every detail of the brave's appearance in his mind. He was about twenty-five, short and stockily built. He had a nondescript face, except for an old knife scar running up from the corner of his mouth to just beneath his right eye. He sported just one feather at the back of

111

his head, and in addition to the top part of Elizabeth's dress, he wore buckskin pants. His feet were bare.

"I'm talking to you," the sub-chief said, jabbing the muzzle of the Winchester painfully into Edge's hip to bring him back to full awareness of where he was.

Edge's lips curled back to show an evil grin. "But you ain't saying nothing good, uh?"

The sub-chief eyed him levelly. "Black Hawk wants to know why you came here?"

Edge raised a hand to point to the scar-faced brave. The Indian realized he had suddenly become the center of attention and tried to draw back. But the press of bodies around him trapped him where he was. His eyes showed fear as he looked everywhere but at the ice-cold expression on Edge's face. "To kill him?"

Black Hawk glanced at the brave indicated, and grimaced at the fear he showed. "Why you want kill Silent Thunder?" he demanded.

"Kidnapped my wife," Edge answered, still staring at the trembling brave. "Probably killed her, since he's wearing part of her frock."

Black Hawk unfolded his arms and crooked a finger towards Silent Thunder. The brave stepped forward, and came to a trembling halt when the chief extended his hand, palm forward.

"You're invited to question him," the sub-chief explained, his good humor returning, shown by a wry smile.

Edge raked his eyes over the crowd and saw a great many similar smiles. "He go to the same school you did?"

112

The sub-chief shook his head, rustling the feathers. "No, a lousy agency class. Never could speak English good. Can't speak it at all now. Can't even speak Siouan. Told a bad lie one time. Pretended to have great courage, but proved a coward. Used to be called Rolling Thunder. Black Hawk's great-uncle, Sitting Bull, personally cut out tongue and gave new name."

The brave hung his head in shame as the story of his disgrace and punishment was retold. Edge eyed him with dispassion. "He ever get caught with another man's squaw?" he asked sourly.

"Only tongue taken from him," came the reply. "Whole man everywhere else."

Again Edge had to force back the anger, blotting out the threatened image of Elizabeth's terror in the hands of the mute, scar-faced brave. "There were a whole bunch of braves at my place," he said. "I don't give a damn which one tells it, but I want to know what happened to my wife."

Native cruelty swept away the good-humor. "She's past worrying about. None of the raiding parties brought back prisoners." The grin he showed now was an evil leer. "She wouldn't have died easy, but she'd have died loved."

Edge knew he had no chance of reaching the scar-faced brave. But the sub-chief was close at hand and the half-breed was filled with enough hate to swamp the entire Sioux nation. One moment he was stock still, seemingly transfixed by the weight of his emotion. But then he whirled, arms rising and hands curled. The metal of the rifle barrel was cool against his sweat-sticky palms. He heard a gasp from the watching Indians, and the dry clicks of a score of

113

bullets being pumped into breeches. Then, as he forced the Winchester's muzzle out of line with his body, Black Hawk's voice barked a command. He tensed himself for the thud of lead into his body, but the silence which followed the chief's order was unbroken by gunfire.

The sub-chief allowed the rifle to be forced down so far and no more. The effort it took to withstand the pressure of Edge's strength showed as only a tautness of his facial skin. His eyes met those of the half-breed's over a distance of less than two feet. They sparkled with the intent to kill.

"Black Hawk says leave you to me," he hissed between clenched teeth. "May the best man win, uh?"

"I always do," Edge rasped, and jerked back on the rifle.

He had been holding it out to his side, on a level with his hip. As he yanked it, he pivoted on the ball of one foot and thudded his shoulder forward and up. It crashed home to the Indian's jaw, crunching his teeth together as he opened his mouth to hurl a retort. The surprise blow hurt the Indian, but not enough to make him release his grip on the stock and lever of the rifle. He revealed his pain with just a low grunt, then countered. He fell backwards, retaining his hold on the rifle so that Edge was forced to follow him. Both his moccasined feet swept up as he hit the ground. Edge saw what was happening, but could do nothing about it. The Indian's feet thudded agonizingly into his stomach and he had to go where the thrust of the kick and his own momentum carried him. His body cartwheeled high into the air and then swung down. He heard a throaty roar of approval from the watchers as he crashed, full-length on to his back. A gasp of pain ripped from his lips as the base of his spine took the full impact of the fall.

The moon seemed to zig-zag across the sky, dodging crazily among the stars. But the hallucination lasted only a moment. He shook free of it and rolled over, thrusting up his arms to point the rifle skywards. The Indian had also forced himself into a roll, a wicked grin splitting his lips as he saw Edge's head only inches away from the rifle muzzle. But at the moment he squeezed the trigger, Edge forced up the barrel. The crack of the shot cut across the babble of the excited crowd. The bullet whined up into the night sky.

The Indian emitted a growl of disgust and released his hold on the rifle, using both hands to help power his spring upright. Edge experienced no elation. He had the rifle, but his grip was on the barrel and the lever needed to be pumped. Even before he was on his haunches, the sub-chief, self-assurance replacing his disappointment, had drawn a knife with a nine-inch blade. The Indian lunged forward, the knife slashing through the air. Edge sprang upwards and backwards, sweeping up the rifle as a club. The Indian howled as the stock cracked against his wrist, deflecting the knife thrust. The knife fell from numbed fingers and Edge started to turn the Winchester. But the sub-chief caught the knife neatly in his left hand and leapt forward, arm at full-length, the point of the weapon aimed at the half-breed's heart.

Edge pivoted and leaned backwards from the waist. The angle of the knife blade was altered with a simple twist of the wrist. Triumphant joy masked the Indian's face. A thousand voices were raised in

115

anticipation of the kill. By changing his grip on the rifle, Edge had reduced its effectiveness as a club. But it became a defensive shield. When the knife had less than two inches to travel before it plunged into him he jerked the Winchester up, across his body. The power of the Indian's thrust drove the knife deep into the rosewood stock of the rifle.

Those watchers standing behind Edge had no way of knowing the knife had not plunged into his body. A roar of triumph went up from this section of the audience and they waited expectantly for the half-breed to stagger back with blood spurting from his chest. Instead, Edge continued with the pivoting motion. Unwilling to release his hold on a second weapon, the sub-chief found himself halted abruptly in his forward leap. He thudded flat-footed to the ground, and was then hurled back and to the side. The power of Edge's sweeping turn and the whip action of the rifle hurled the Indian into a backwards stagger as he was forced to relinquish his grip on the knife handle.

The roar died, merging into the stunned silence with which those able to see the move had greeted the sub-chief's failure to kill Edge. The Indian flailed his arms, but was unable to maintain his balance. He sat down hard, his body whipping backwards, to be halted abruptly as he banged against the legs of the stony-faced Black Hawk. The chief, and the entire audience, fixed the defeated man with a contemptuous stare.

Edge used the momentary respite to turn the rifle, with the knife still firmly stuck into the stock. Not until the Winchester made its ominous clicking

116

of ejection and cocking did he regain the attention of every eye in the camp.

"Kill him," Black Hawk instructed in a funereal tone, refolding his arms, "Such battle is to the death. It is Sioux custom."

Edge was aiming the rifle negligently at the disgraced sub-chief, who showed shame but no fear. "Is it also custom to blast me as soon as I squeeze this trigger?" he asked evenly.

He could see only a section of the silent Indians, with less than half a dozen rifles aimed at him. But he could sense the menacing muzzles of many other guns directed towards him.

"Not for him," Black Hawk rasped, bending one knee and thudding it into the back of the sub-chief's head. "We saw fair fight. But no way knowing how you killed three braves on hill."

Edge clicked his tongue against the back of his bared teeth and shook his head. "I ain't buying that," he replied evenly. "Reckon I'll take *my* custom elsewhere."

As he spoke, he elevated the aim of the rifle and his pose was no longer casual. The stock, with the knife protruding to the side, nestled against his shoulder. One eye closed and the other narrowed to a glinting slit. He flicked up the back sight with a finger and drew a bead on the center of Black Hawk's head.

"Figure you're in charge of the store, feller," he said. "You ready to put up the shutters or do we do a deal?"

Black Hawk blinked. It was the only sign of his surprise. Whispered conversation scratched the night's stillness, but it was succeeded only by more

117

silence. No one was prepared to act without a command from the chief.

"You fool. You still die."

"I reckon," Edge allowed. "But I'd rather go to the Happy Hunting Ground with you than him. Full chief's just got to have more influence up there than a sub-chief. And the way things have been, I figure I'll need someone with pull to get me through the pearly gates."

Black Hawk was not sure he understood everything Edge said. But he fully appreciated the meaning of the unwavering aim of the Winchester.

"What you want?"

Edge spat from the corner of his mouth. "Out of here."

The chief pondered a moment, then fired off a burst of throaty sounds which comprised instructions in his own language. The sub-chief glanced up at Edge's resolute expression behind the rifle and the look on his own face revealed his low estimate of the half-breed's chances.

"I will walk ahead of you to last teepees in camp," Black Hawk told Edge. "Braves not kill you unless you harm me."

"No deal," Edge replied immediately. "I take you to the ridge or the butte. And I take a pony."

Black Hawk frowned as he considered these requests. The braves waited. The fires crackled. He shook his head, then nodded. "Pony you have. I come only to last teepees."

"Tell 'em," Edge said.

Another short burst of Siouan was directed to the frustrated audience of Indians. One brave moved out of the crowd to the rear, and broke into a run towards the drystone wall corral. Black Hawk stepped backwards, but only a pace. It showed his confidence in the marksmanship of his braves. Forty rifles cracked in perfect synchronization when the chief dropped his hands to his sides. The sub-chief had been expecting the end and offered no futile resistance. Every bullet drilled into his head, each killing impact countering the effect of another. So that, for stretched seconds, he teetered in his sitting position, a man without a head: just a blood-dripping skull. Then, as pieces of torn flesh and gristle flew away from him to spray over a wide area, he toppled to the side. One miraculously still-perfect brown eye, like an oddly colored egg, surveyed his executioners with mild surprise. Out of the other socket oozed dark brain matter, with the consistency and hue of fresh mud.

Black Hawk eyed Edge balefully. "Him endanger my life," he explained. "Indian law—for that he must pay."

"Sure, chief," Edge answered, holding the Indian's level gaze along the length of the Winchester's barrel. "For something as bad as that, he's just gotta be liable to get Siouxed."

CHAPTER ELEVEN

Silently, as Edge circled around to stand behind Black Hawk, the Indians reformed themselves into two close-packed rows, marking a path towards the southern fringe of the camp. When they were in position the hatred generated by every brave and squaw seemed to be a palpable force, designed to provoke the white man into making a fatal error.

But the half-breed was no stranger to this tactic. He possessed the ability himself and used it as a weapon—the glinting eyes in a frozen face that spoke a clearer threat than a thousand harsh words.

The brave who had brought the pony from the corral headed first down the human corridor. Edge allowed him to have a start of twenty feet.

"Okay, chief, move it," he rasped. "And hope the guys in the bleachers remember I've declared open season on birds of any color."

Black Hawk moved forward with great dignity, arms held akimbo again and face set in an expression of firmly controlled anger. Edge trailed him, the Winchester still aimed from the shoulder with the muzzle a constant foot away from the back of the proudly held head. Moonlight glinted on the blade of the knife projecting at right angles from the stock. But Edge's narrowed eye behind the back sight gleamed with a greater intensity. His knuckle was white around the trigger.

As he came level with each flanking pair of braves, the Indians brought up their rifles to an equally steady aim. But Edge gave them only one opportunity for a snap shot that might have killed him before he could blast a bullet into Black Hawk's head. This was when he glanced for a split-second at the scar-faced brave who wore proof of his complicity in Elizabeth's abduction. But if the Indian riflemen closest to Edge saw that he was fleetingly distracted, they were unprepared to match their speed with his.

The brave led the pony a few feet out into the open from between the tail end of the two lines of tense watchers. There he halted and turned around.

"We stop here," Black Hawk said, but merely shortened his stride.

"When I say," Edge rasped in reply, readjusting his pace to that of the chief. He made his captive walk about ten yards clear of the camp. Then: "Okay, halt and turn around."

As Black Hawk complied, Edge side-stepped in a half circle, placing the chief between himself and the silent watchers.

"You leave now!" Black Hawk commanded.

"When I get what I came for," Edge snarled. "Tell the stable boy to bring scarface out here."

"I not know what you mean."

"I want Silent Thunder," Edge demanded.

"Not part of agreement," the chief retorted with great determination. "You not to be trusted in making deal."

Edge sent a stream of spit out of the corner of his

121

mouth. "I wouldn't buy a used wagon from you, either. Do like I said."

"No!" As he barked his reply, the chief's back became ramrod stiff, his shoulders rising as he filled his lungs with what he thought might be his last breath.

"You tired of living, feller," Edge asked evenly, not revealing in his tone that he sensed defeat.

"I do not send brave to certain death only to save my life, pale face. You insist, we both tired of living. Sleep together."

"Thanks, but you're not the kind of bird I fancy," the half-breed replied, knowing that Black Hawk was not bluffing.

"What do now?"

"Turn around again."

The chief did so.

"Tell him to give you the pony."

Black Hawk chose to stare down the bore of the Winchester rather than focus on Edge's face. "I said only this far." His tone was adamant.

Edge's voice was as hard as mahogany granite. "So tell the boys to start shooting," he rasped. "If I turn you loose inside rifle range I'm dead anyway."

The chief's reply was a short sentence of Siouan. The nervous brave approached him slowly, passed over the rope bridle than scuttled hurriedly back to join the audience. Edge would have preferred to keep the chief and the rest of the tribe in view, but it would have meant him walking backwards. And he could not afford a stumble. So he side-stepped around another half-circle.

"Nice and easy, feller," he instructed.

Black Hawk started forward. Edge moved off in

his wake with the length of the pony between them. A thousand pairs of moccasined feet shuffled along behind him.

"Don't think the boys and girls have got the idea," Edge hissed.

The chief barked out a single syllable and the Indians halted. Edge's arms were aching from holding the Winchester in the same position for so long. His hands were sticky with the sweat of stress and there were dark stains on his tattered shirt. But with each pace, widening the gap between his itching back and the levelled rifles of the braves Edge's discomfort lessened. But then, when he and his prisoner were well advanced up the slope towards the ridge, relaxation of tension became a threat. A delayed reaction to his lack of proper rest over so many hours combined with the painful gnaw of hunger to assault him with weakness. The headdress of the chief became a colorful blur. His legs seemed to be fastened with hanging weights. A buzzing like the sound of a thousand hornets filled his skull. He felt ready to drop in his tracks. But the itch between his shoulder blades became a pressure point, as if he could actually feel the weight of the many guns against his flesh. This prodded him into fighting the fatigue.

"How far?" Black Hawk grunted.

"Top'll be fine," Edge replied.

"We still catch up with you. You bring disgrace on Black Hawk. Must be avenged. You suffer real bad."

Edge ignored the threat. Talking disturbed his concentration. The chief's voice seemed to float in to him from a great distance and his own words had

123

a detached quality in his ears. He gritted his teeth and snapped open both eyes to their fullest extent. He saw only the feathered headdress, which appeared to be floating along in front of him on a sea of blackness which blotted out everything else from his consciousness. But suddenly the chief stopped. Edge halted automatically. He glanced to left and right, then over his shoulder. They had arrived at the top of the rise. The camp fires below were distant pin-pricks of red and orange. The Indians had clustered into one enormous group. The moonlight shone on their upturned faces.

"You did a good job," Edge told Black Hawk, who was immobile, with his back still turned to the halfbreed.

"Sioux are patient people," the chief said. "We wait."

"I always tip a waiter," Edge told him, lifted his right leg and kicked out.

The toe of his boot caught the Indian chief in the small of the back and he lurched forward with a cry of alarm. He saw the lip of a ledge before him and unfolded his arms to beat at the air. The rope bridle slipped from his hand and Edge reached out and caught it as the pony reared. Black Hawk's body was canted too far forward and his momentum was too great for him to save himself. He went head first off the ledge, cartwheeled once on the almost perpendicular cliff-face and thudded to a crushing stop twenty feet below.

A roar of rage exploded from the massed Indians at the foot of the butte, masking the groans of the chief as he stared at the jagged point of his fractured right femur jutting from his thigh.

"Pale face speak with forked tongue!" he bellowed.

Rifle fire sounded from the camp, some of the Indians crouching to aim at the out-of-range target while others broke away at a run towards the corral. Edge swung a long leg over the back of the pony and thudded in his heels, urging the animal off the ledge and down a natural pathway.

"Black Hawk birdbrain to believe!" he yelled as the hoots and hollers of warcries rose from the camp.

He rode as fast as he dared down the rugged slope, guessing that the Sioux brave would not have cut out the best pony from the corral. But the animal was sure-footed enough, ignoring certain jerks on the reins when his own horse sense and sharp eye showed him a safer turn than that indicated by his rider. His weakness showed up on the comparatively flat terrain stretching so many miles towards the forest in the south. He moved well through a trot into a canter, but the promise was not fulfilled when he reached a gallop. He snorted and strained, game to give what his rider demanded, but incapable of the speed Edge needed to outrun the Indians.

Being astride a horse eased the half-breed's physical fatigue. And he could relegate the need to satisfy hunger to its proper position in the priorities. But the insect-like buzzing continued to fill his head and the blur of speed which was spread over the ground immediately beneath the pony's pumping hooves extended to the horizon on all sides. So that, when he glanced over his shoulder, the mass of mounted Sioux racing down the side of the butte seemed as one with the gigantic outcrop, as if the rock and earth had turned to seething, boiling mud.

"Bastards killed Beth!" he yelled at himself. "Gotta get him before they get me."

There had been a score or more braves who raided the cabin and carried his wife away. To be certain he wrought vengeance upon all of those responsible, he would have to kill every brave in the Sioux nation— be they Santee, Teton or Yankton. That was impossible. So he channelled every iota of his hate towards the tongueless Indian who had appropriated her dress. He was the one who would have to pay for all of them. He fixed in his desperately weary mind a vivid image of the brave's viciously scarred face and it was this mental exercise which held him on the bare back of the pony—kept him from slumping to the rushing ground, senseless, in the path of the enraged Indians who pursued him.

But something more was needed if he was to survive the headlong chase and live to carry out what he had to do. For relentlessly, with every yard covered by the struggling pony, the shrieking braves were overhauling the white man. He did not look back to see them, but the increasing volume of their high-pitched warcries was evidence enough that they were closing up on him. And the absence of rifle fire told of their intention to capture him alive: Black Hawk's order that all whites should be slaughtered without delay obviously did not apply to Edge.

At night, the terrain presented a bleaker prospect than it had during the blazing heat of the day. For the shadows thrown by the pale moonlight seemed somehow more menacing and with no shimmering

126

haze clinging to the ground the horizons retreated, enlarging the desolate wasteland and emphasizing the lack of adequate cover. Blurred eyesight, which occasionally cleared and just as often expanded into double vision, added greatly to Edge's desperate situation.

It was during a period of receiving dual images as he crouched low on the pony, clinging to the stretched neck, that he first saw the soldiers. They were mounted cavalry and there seemed to be a whole battalion of them, grouped at the top of a slight rise a mile or so ahead.

Edge was certain it was an hallucination. He screwed his eyes tight shut and held them so for long seconds. In the self-imposed pitch darkness, the screams and warcries of the Sioux swelled to enormous volume. He tightened his already vise-like grip on the Winchester and tensed himself for the impact when the leading brave leapt at him and knocked him to the ground.

But as the seconds were stretched into hours by the struggling forces of hate, torment and exhaustion in his broiling mind, his headlong dash continued unabated. He started to open his eyes, cracking them against the sting of rushing air. The warcries faded, became faint and ceased. His eyes took in a crystally-clear vista of a twelve-man patrol, jerking from a halt into a full gallop.

He pulled himself upright and twisted his head. He thought every brave in the camp had been sent in pursuit of him. But there were less than twenty of them. They had seen the horse soldiers at the same time as Edge, and slowed to consider the new situation with its changed odds.

127

Rifle fire exploded against the background rumble of shod and unshod hooves. It was the soldiers who had opened up, their bullets whining close by Edge's head. He went into a low crouch on the pony again, expecting to hear an answering fusillade which would put him in a deadly crossfire. But it didn't happen. The group of Sioux split into two sections and veered away in opposite directions. One brave was hurled from his pony, his hip wound proving fatal as his head smashed against the ground, snapping his neck. The other braves in both groups completed a full circle and merged again, racing away, back towards the twin-peaked butte.

"We got 'em on the run!" a young trooper yelled excitedly, exploding a useless bullet towards the retreating Indians as they galloped out of range. "Scared the crap outa 'em."

As Edge hauled on the reins, bringing the snorting pony to a halt, he doubted that the trooper's jubilation was based on a correct guess. For under normal circumstances a score of Sioux would have considered themselves more than adequate in a pitched battle with a dozen horse-soldiers. But caught in the middle was Edge, the man Black Hawk wanted alive—and the Sioux chief was too far away to offer guidance under the fresh set of circumstances.

Edge slid from the pony and sat down hard as the animal skidded to a stop. He drew in great gasps of air and tried to yank the knife from the Winchester stock. His inability to complete this simple task revealed the extent of his weakness.

He gave up and waited for the soldiers to arrive, choking and coughing on the dust raised by the sliding and stamping hooves of their horses. The patrol was under the command of a fresh-faced captain with eager eyes and a jutting jawline. There was one sergeant and the rest were enlisted men. They looked curiously down at Edge seated on the ground at the side of the pony. He had lost his hat and his long hair was matted and coated with dust. Crystals of dried sweat salt made highlights in the long stubble of his lower face. His pants were ripped over the right knee and his shirt was in ribbons. Exhaustion showed in every sagging line of his lean face and muscular body. But his unbroken spirit glinted through his hooded eyes as he curled back his lips in a grin.

"Obliged, feller," he said to the officer.

The youngster saluted smartly. "Captain Booth at your service sir. Like to ask you some questions."

"Ought to promote you," Edge muttered, massaging his forehead as he suddenly saw two officers astride two horses.

"Beg pardon, sir?" Booth asked with a quizzical look at the half-breed.

Edge closed his eyes and sighed. "Ought to be a general," he mumbled. "Army sure brought this sinner salvation."

He toppled sideways into warm unconsciousness.

CHAPTER TWELVE

The captain was torn between leaving a man to take care of Edge and leading the others in pursuit of the band of Sioux, or making a strategic withdrawal from the area. For the orders given by his commanding officer were not precise when applied to this situation. His job was to patrol deep into the broken plain to try to spot and estimate the strength of Sioux concentrations. He was supposed to avoid clashes and in the event of an unprovoked attack, to follow a course by which the safety of himself and his men was at least risk.

The sighting of twenty braves who had unaccountably turned tail and ran merited further investigation. But it was the possibility that the Sioux had taken off to fetch reinforcements which finally settled the decision for him. Out here in open country with such sparse cover, his men were at high risk.

He tried to rouse the unconscious Edge, but without success. The half-breed had a lot of exhaustion to shed in the warm darkness of deep sleep before his mind was prepared to admit the cold light of waking.

His decision made, Captain Booth wasted little time in implementing it. The Indian pony was abandoned to wander at will, while two troopers lifted Edge's inert form and slung it across the sergeant's horse, forward of the saddle. Then, with all the men remounted, the order was given to move out, and a single column was formed. The captain was at the head and set a cantering pace. The sergeant rode immediately behind the officer, cursing under his breath as he struggled to stay on station while having to constantly readjust the limp form of Edge to keep him from sliding to the ground.

Back marker was the young trooper who had been so filled with joy at the sight of the fleeing Sioux. But now his mood had undergone a drastic change. He had been told a lot of horrifying tales about the artfulness of Indians. What if the band of Sioux had tricked the captain into believing they were retreating? They could be moving up again, stealthily and silently—and riding at the rear of the column, he was sure to be the first soldier killed.

The column kept up a hard, relentless pace, angling towards the southwest throughout the entire night. Then the grayness of a new day put out feelers across the dark sky, like probing fingers which discovered it was possible to dim the bright dots of stars and pale the moon into insignificance. Soon, when this advance attack proved successful, the big guns of the sun exploded from the eastern horizon.

Captain Booth ordered no breakfast stop for in the far distance he could see his objective and he was eager to reach it. He never looked back over his shoulder, confident that the nervous young trooper at the rear was constantly alert and would immediately report if a telltale dust cloud rose in the light of the new day.

He led his men into Fort Wells at eight-thirty and without exception the troopers were grateful that he had forced such a hard pace. Not that the fort itself offered very much in the way of security from Indian attack. It consisted of one large headquarters building constructed of prepared timber and a half dozen bunkhouses built of rough hewn logs, the whole set in a compound bounded by a roughly circular trench with the displaced earth piled around the outer rim. Planks of timber were rested across the trench at one point, to allow the patrol into the compound, and removed when the horses had clattered over the bridge. But although the fort could not be termed a stronghold, at least it was manned by thirty more troopers and two officers. The members of the patrol were very pleased to see their comrades.

Fort Wells was sited on the fringe of the forest twenty miles west of the point where the Sioux had led Edge out of the timber. Its sole purpose was to monitor Indian activity on the rugged plain spread to the north and relate reports to Fort James which lay forty miles to the south. It was, in fact, a patrol from Wells which had first spotted the signs of a massing of Sioux strength.

Edge came out of his stupor as the fort's only medical orderly stooped over him to force brandy between his lips. The half-breed's throat constricted against the burning liquid and he was certain he was being choked. He snapped open his eyes and saw the blurred shape of a man towering over him with both

132

arms stretching out towards him. In a lightning re-flex action, the urge to survive overriding his weak-ness, he streaked a hand to the back of his neck. But the familiar smooth wood of the razor handle protruding from the pouch was not there. This lack triggered his memory to summon total recall of ev-erything that had happened to him. He blinked and his vision cleared. He recognized the uniform shirt of a soldier, and saw the expression of naked fear on the young orderly's face.

"I look that bad, trooper?" he croaked, glancing around him.

He was lying, fully dressed, on top of the covers of a cot in a tiny sick bay. There was another cot in there, but it was empty.

"Christ, mister," the orderly gasped. "You looked ready to kill me."

Edge showed his icy grin and took the tumbler from the man's trembling hands. He gulped the brandy at a single swallow and then allowed his head to fall back on to the pillow. "Looks can't kill, trooper," he said. "And looking's about all I feel up to right now. But if your food's only half as good as your liquor, I won't even glance at you—if that makes you feel any better."

"There's some soup on the way," the orderly an-swered. "Major Schmitt's anxious you be strong enough to talk as soon as possible."

"Obliged to the major for thinking about my wel-fare," Edge said cynically, pushing his legs off the side of the bed and sitting up.

The orderly made a move to restrain him, but sensed that his patient was the kind of man determined to do whatever he wanted to and would not take

133

kindly to advice. Edge didn't have to stand up to see through the window. From the bed he could see a wide view of the compound and a stretch of the perimeter trench and earth wall. A dozen troopers had their backs to him, resting their rifles across the heap of dirt and scanning the sun-baked plain to the north.

A cook corporal brought in a bowl of beef broth and some sourdough biscuits and Edge was halfway through eating the meal when Captain Booth entered with his commanding officer. Schmitt was a big, broad-chested man in his late forties with weary eyes and a crooked mouth. Anxiety showed in every line of his squarish face.

"How are you feeling?" he asked as if he didn't care.

"Alive," Edge answered.

Schmitt nodded his bullet head in curt acknowledgement. "What were you doing out there in Indian land?" he demanded.

Edge chewed on a chunk of tough beef. "Looking for Indians," he replied, and saw the flush of anger tint the major's deeply-tanned complexion. "Ones that kidnapped my wife."

It dampened Schmitt's threatened anger. "See anything before you ran into the bunch that was after you?"

Edge continued to eat, emptying his mouth before replying. "Nothing good. A thousand or more are camped north of the twin-peaked butte."

The major and the captain exchanged dour glances. "They in a fighting mood?" the senior officer wanted to know.

"Painted like fourth of July, feathered better than

134

full grown buzzards and clawed with Winchesters fresh out of the plant."

Schmitt gave another of his short nods. "Thank you. Rest now. If I'm ordered to hold this fort, I'll need every able-bodied man I can get."

He went out of the sick bay, closely followed by Booth. The orderly held back for a few moments, but received no encouragement from the still-eating Edge and he left, too. He neglected, by design or otherwise, to remove the bottle of French brandy. So when Edge had finished the meal, he topped it with another drink. After that he rolled and smoked a cigarette and tested his weight on his legs. He was far short of the peak of physical fitness, but as he paced the small room he could feel his muscles reacting to the effects of food and exercise.

From the window, at one end of the headquarters building, he saw a mounted trooper receive a dispatch pouch from Major Schmitt. The planks were placed across the trench and the rider clattered across. He half circled the perimeter and galloped off into the trees behind the fort.

From close to the window, the half-breed could see that a guard of twenty men were positioned in the northern arc of the trench. He looked across their heads and narrowed his eyes to survey the seemingly endless wilderness which held the men's intense concentration. Heat shimmer severely shortened the range of vision, but he guessed there would be ample warning of a Sioux attack.

He stretched out on the cot. Less than a minute later, when the orderly knocked and entered with a bowl of hot water and a fresh army-issue shirt and pants, he discovered the half-breed was soundly

135

asleep. Having no wish to test the man's amazingly fast reflexes again, he placed his burdens on a dresser and withdrew. Edge came close to waking, sensed he was alone again, and sank back down the curve into a deep sleep.

It was midday when the bugle call snapped him into full awareness. He rolled off the cot and reached the window in two strides. More than a score of troopers, some in shirt sleeves and others struggling into tunics, were running across the compound to reinforce the men already in the trench. Three of them staggered under the weight of the component parts of a Gatling gun, which they started to set up at a central point on the northern perimeter. As the last man thudded down into the trench, the bugler abruptly ended the call. The sounds of the rapid-fire gun being snapped together were all that disturbed the stillness.

For the advancing Sioux were holding their peace.

They were still more than three miles out across the wasteland, stretched out in a line almost a mile wide. How many ranks there were was impossible to tell, for the heat shimmer drifted across the arid terrain in waves, shrouding the Indians as effectively as an autumn morning mist.

"Major's compliments, sir," the orderly said in a rush as he opened the door. "He'd appreciate it if you'd join him on the compound."

The man was fully-dressed in uniform now, and carried a Winchester. Edge turned and nodded in acknowledgment. His own rifle rested in a corner, with a knife still firmly stuck in the stock. He wrenched it free with ease as he followed the orderly down a

136

corridor and through a doorway into the full, dazzling harshness of the noon sun.

Schmitt and Booth, with a lieutenant, formed a small group in front of the headquarters building. As the orderly ran to take up a position in the trench, the major finished a surveillance of the enemy through binoculars. His face was tense as he handed them to Edge.

"Your estimate was a little short," he accused.

Edge took the binoculars and raised them to his hooded eyes. He focussed on one end of the line of advance and the lenses brought a group of vividly-painted braves into seeming touching distance. He swept the glasses along the entire line and counted six chiefs, two of them Cheyenne. One of the Sioux chiefs was Black Hawk, his broken leg bound and splinted, stretching out stiffly from the side of his pony. There were at least ten rows of mounted braves behind the leading line. Dust and shimmer clouded the rear.

"I reckon three thousand I can see," Edge said as he handed back the binoculars. "That's three times as many as I saw last night, major. Weren't no Cheyenne out at the twin-peaked butte."

"Waiting to join up with the others," the lieutenant said nervously.

"Didn't have to wait long," Edge put in, shading his eyes to stare out at the Sioux.

"Know anything about Indian fighting, mister?" Schmitt asked.

Edge spat into the dust and began to reload the Winchester from the diminishing stock of shells in his pants pockets. "They're like everybody else," he answered wryly. "Kill 'em and they don't get up."

137

The major grimaced. He had spent a great part of his army life on isolated posts with the minimum of contact with civilians. He was not used to—and did not like—Edge's lack of respect for his rank.

"Just like that, uh?"

Edge pushed the final shell in through the gate and showed his cold grin to the major. Then he glanced across the heads of the troopers again. "Naturally, it's easier when there aren't so many of 'em coming at you."

Schmitt cleared his throat, conscious of the gaze of the captain and lieutenant, who obviously expected him to bawl out the arrogant civilian. But with the Sioux drawing closer by the moment, he realized this was neither the time nor the place to waste anger on a man fate had decreed to be his ally. "Unless I receive orders to the contrary, I intend to do all in my power to hold this position mister," he rasped.

Edge turned a full three hundred and sixty degrees, his expression showing his dissatisfaction with what he saw. Open ground on three sides and dense timber on the other. In the middle, a comparative handful of men with only the trench and insubstantial timber buildings for cover.

"Very noble," the half-breed commented.

"Are you with us?" Schmitt asked.

Edge looked at Booth. "I owe the captain," he replied. "For a couple of drinks, a few hours sleep and a meal. Guess men have died for less."

Neither Schmitt nor the junior officer could think of an answer for that, and Edge broke away from the group and crossed to the trench. He dropped down into it and found himself between the orderly

138

and the sergeant who had carried him in from the plain.

"Ordered to stay, uh?" the squint-eyed non-com muttered, nestling his cheek against the stock of his Winchester.

"Nobody gives me orders," Edge answered, leaning forward against the heap of earth and sighting along his own rifle.

"So why didn't you take off through the timber?" the orderly asked. "Have your pick of the horses. Don't reckon any of us will need 'em anymore."

"Guy out there I want," the half-breed said as the three officers split up and took their battle stations—Booth on the left flank, the lieutenant on the right and Schmitt in the center.

"Only one?" the sergeant asked wryly as the Sioux advance halted, a few yards out of rifle range.

The soldiers waited, bodies tense, fingers curled around triggers, tanned faces pale and sheened by sweat. The dust raised by the Sioux ponies settled and it seemed, in the utter silence, that the men in the trench could hear the settling of each tiny mote.

"Ain't greedy," Edge muttered against the stillness.

"You can take as many of these cookies as you want, mister," the non-com whispered, swatting at a buzzing fly. "Plenty for everybody."

Edge drew the Sioux knife from his pants' waistband and thrust it into the dirt. "Obliged, but I wouldn't want to get toothache," he answered.

"Uh?"

A piercing whistle shrilled: and signalled an explosion of full-throated warcries as the Indians heeled their ponies into a charge.

"I want revenge, and that's supposed to be sweet," Edge rasped as he narrowed his eye behind the backsight. He squeezed the trigger and a brave was toppled from his pony, pouring blood from a head wound.

The sergeant, like the other soldiers, was waiting for the order to fire. "That him?" he yelled as Edge pumped the Winchester's action.

"Ain't that easy," the half-breed answered and fired again, hitting a pony, which rolled and bucked its rider into the path of the trampling hooves following. "But I reckon I can stand the pain for as long as it takes me to get a drilling and lead filling."

"Fire!" Schmitt roared.

CHAPTER THIRTEEN

The Sioux chief leading the first attacking wave of braves issued the same order to his followers simultaneously with the cavalry major. The warcries of the Indians were almost drowned out by the sharp crackle of more than a hundred rifles, and in the next instant became mingled with the screams of the wounded.

The attackers were shrouded in billowing clouds of dust and appeared as merely black shadows in the swirling gray. But the men in the trenches had the satisfaction of seeing several loose ponies spurt ahead as they became unburdened of dead or wounded riders.

Three of the defenders slumped forward across the earth and then slid down into the foot of the trench, one of them pouring blood from a hole where his left eye had once been, another crying for his mother as he tried to staunch the flow of scarlet from the side of his neck and the third screaming and swatting at flies which zoomed in to feed on his bullet torn cheek.

Gunsmoke drifted along the trench, dropping its acrid stench over the men as they pumped a hair of lead towards the rapidly closing dust cloud, spitting death back at them.

Edge fired, ducked low to pump the Winchester's action, rose and fired again. On each fleeting occasion that his slitted eyes peered across the mound of earth, the impossibility of defending the fort was made more apparent.

For only the center group of Indians were attacking; and probably just the first few ranks of these. The flanks of the joint Sioux-Cheyenne force were moving up slowly and it was highly likely that there was a backup body of braves covering the center should the initial attack fail.

He counted his twelfth shot and crouched down low in the trench, digging fresh ammunition from a carton at the feet of the sergeant. The Gatling began to chatter its own brand of indiscriminate death and a cheer went up from the soldiers as they saw the effect of the spewing bullets spraying along the line of advance.

"We're murderin' 'em!" the orderly shrieked. He opened his mouth to vent a burst of jubilant laughter.

An arrow hissed out of the dust and splatted into the back of his throat. He was thrown against the rear wall of the trench and slid down into a sitting position. Death drained the joy from his staring eyes.

"Should have kept your mouth shut," Edge said to the unresponsive face, springing upright and squeezing the trigger as soon as he had a clear shot.

A brave had galloped to within four feet of the trench, and leapt clear of his mount, a tomahawk swinging up. The half-breed's shot took him in the groin. He screamed and slumped across the mound of earth, head hanging into the trench. The sergeant snatched up his fallen tomahawk and thudded it into the back of the brave's neck.

"That sure give him the chop!" he roared triumphantly as the severed head dropped into the trench.

At the center of the line, four braves hurled themselves from their ponies, revolvers blazing and knives flashing. The Gatling gun was silenced and the blood from its two man crew hissed as it sprayed from gaping wounds on to hot metal.

A brave loomed up on the dirt mound in front of the sergeant, and he swung the tomahawk again, letting go of the handle. The axe spun once between the brave's legs. Then the blade sank deep into the Indian's crotch. His scream seemed to blot out every other sound of the fierce battle.

"He sings soprano good!" the non-com bellowed.

As the brave toppled forward, he managed to bring up his revolver and squeeze the trigger. The sergeant gasped, swayed, and crumpled, the Indian falling across him in the bottom of the trench. Blood and a darker liquid oozed from a hole in the top of his head.

"Ain't only the high notes he can hit," Edge muttered, whirling towards a sound behind him.

The attacking brave thrust forward with a knife. The Winchester cracked and the brave was flung backwards, gouting blood from his heart. Behind his falling body, around the curving trench, more blood spurted, accompanied by the screams of white men and Indians as they fought to the death at close quarters. In the other direction, it was the same.

143

Corpses, in army blue and buckskin, littered the mound of earth and bottom of the trench in myriad attitudes of death.

Beyond the fort's pathetically inadequate defensive line, the charge was over. The dust floated gently to earth, finely coating the inert forms of braves and ponies and thickening the drying blood which had spilled from their wounds.

The painted face of a brave appeared at the top of the mound immediately in front of Edge. The half-breed had no time to lever a fresh shell into the Winchester's breech. A revolver pointed at him—single shot and not cocked. He dropped the rifle and swung his arm. He grasped the hair of the Indian and dragged him over the hump of earth. His other hand jerked the knife from the dirt. In the instant before he thrust the knife deep into the gaping mouth of the Indian, he saw through the streaks of warpaint on the face and knew there would be no tongue to hinder the path of the blade—the scar stood out vividly against the sweating skin.

The half-breed's own mouth came open in a roar of jubilation, and his triumph seemed somehow heightened by the warmth of Silent Thunder's blood splashing across his hand. Then the brave's teeth clamped tight on the blade. He slid down into the trench, his body weight straining against Edge's grip on the knife. The half-breed refused to release his hold and the steel blade snapped an inch in front of the hilt.

Edge saw the jagged break and recognized a million-to-one chance of survival. There was no time to check for watching eyes. All he could do was clamp his own teeth around the stump of the blade and force his body to go limp. As he crumpled, he clamped his eyes tight closed. When he hit the bottom of the trench, his head resting against the still warm flesh of a dead brave, he breathed in deeply through his nostrils and trapped the air in his lungs. The blood of Silent Thunder tasted salty.

Within moments, the last surviving soldier assigned to Fort Wells took an arrow through the heart and spilled his blood into the near river soaking into the bottom of the trench.

The two flanks of the Indian advance swung around the sides of the fort and moved into the trees. Those braves who had been engaged in the attack rounded up their ponies and followed. The back-up group caught mounts for the superficially wounded. Those with more serious wounds were left to die: for there was no time or men to spare to care for them.

Edge cracked open his eyes and remained where he had fallen for a full hour after the forest had swallowed up the last braves. Then he rose and climbed out of the trench. At many points along its forward curve, it was filled to overflowing with bodies. There were no longer any wounded: all were dead.

He found his own Winchester with the knife score in the stock, loaded it and refilled his pockets with shells. There were a great many loose horses around, both Indian ponies and cavalry mounts which had broken free of the corral in panic. He selected a strong-looking army gelding and saddled him with tack taken from one of the bunkhouses. The beef stew was luke warm on a cold stove in the cookhouse and he ate a great deal of it. The food filled him and almost masked the after-taste of Silent Thunder's blood in his mouth. Then he took his bearings from the sun and rode into the timber, heading on a route which would bring him to the southern fringe of the forest close to Spear Lake. It also veered him away from the wide path taken by the vengeance seeking Indians.

Edge's own desire for revenge had been satisfied and he rode without haste. He halted only to rest and water the horse during the remainder of the day. But when night came, he stretched out on a patch of lush grass and slept soundly until morning. It was almost noon on the next, equally hot day, when he rode clear of the timber, a few miles to the east of the lake with the cabin on its shore. Within an hour, he rounded the foot of a hill and saw the sparkle of sunlit water. This part of the country was not in the path of the advancing Indians and the little farmstead looked precisely the same as when he had passed by on the trail of the Sioux raiders.

Throughout the entire trek from Fort Wells, he had found it no strain to keep thoughts of Elizabeth at bay. But sight of the cabin brought a thousand and one memories flooding into his mind. As he dismounted in the yard, with its surface still showing stale sign of moccasined feet and unshod hooves, he sensed an emanation of evil rising from the cabin and hovering above it.

But he rejected this image and his movements were precisely determined as he hitched the reins to the picket fence and crossed to the door. It was open and there was a covering of new, undisturbed dust on the step. More dust coated everything in the wrecked living room where he and Elizabeth were married. His boots left marks on the floor as he moved between the smashed furniture and entered the bedroom.

He hesitated in the doorway, seeing the opened cans of blue paint he had bought in Spearville at Elizabeth's request. On one there was a thick skin coating the surface. The other was empty. A brush, with stiffened bristles rested in this. The contents had been applied to one wall.

Edge found he could smile, as he thought of Elizabeth starting to work on painting the room, preparing a surprise for him on his return from town. But then he felt his lips beginning to grow taut as the smile was transformed into a vicious snarl of hate. His vision misted and he knew the blur had nothing to do with exhaustion this time.

He shook his head, clearing his mind of useless emotion, and crossed to the panel concealing the secret hiding place. Inside was almost four thousand dollars. And the neck pouch with the razor, his own Winchester rifle and a gunbelt with a double-action Colt in the holster. If he still had Elizabeth, none of these things would have been important. Without her, they were everything that mattered to him. He pressed the panel at the secret place and it swung open.

Elizabeth fell towards him, more beautiful than he had ever seen her—despite the shapeless denim dress and specks of blue paint on her skin. But beauty is in the eye of the beholder and she was only beautiful to him because he saw her when he thought he never would again.

But as her limp body collapsed into his arms the reality of what had happened to her—what he could have prevented happening—was imprinted into

147

Edge's mind. He had ridden off and left her, the safe hiding place becoming a stifling trap. Her fingers, cleaned of flesh, showed how she had struggled. Her features, contorted by agony, revealed her futile fight for life against the assault of stale air. Then, as her head lolled forward, the stench of the long dead erupted from her gaping mouth. A cluster of writhing maggots fell from her half-eaten lips.

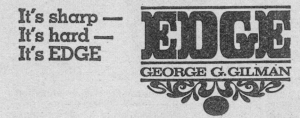

THE "BUTCHER,"
the only man to leave
the Mafia—and live!
A man forever on the run,
unable to trust anyone,
condemned to a life
of constant violence!

THE BUTCHER SERIES

Order		Title	Book #	Price
———	# 1	KILL QUICK OR DIE	P011	.95
———	# 2	COME WATCH HIM DIE	P025	.95
———	# 3	KEEPERS OF DEATH	P603	1.25
———	# 4	BLOOD DEBT	P111	.95
———	# 5	DEADLY DEAL	P152	.95
———	# 6	KILL TIME	P197	.95
———	# 7	DEATH RACE	P228	.95
———	# 8	FIRE BOMB	P608	1.25
———	# 9	SEALED WITH BLOOD	P279	.95
———	#10	THE DEADLY DOCTOR	P291	.95
———	#11	VALLEY OF DEATH	P332	.95
———	#12	KILLER'S CARGO	P429	1.25
———	#13	BLOOD VENGEANCE	P539	1.25
———	#14	AFRICAN CONTRACT	P583	1.25
———	#15	KILL GENTLY, BUT SURE	P671	1.25

AND MORE TO COME . . .

TO ORDER

Please check the space next to the book/s you want, send this order
form together with your check or money order, include the price of
the book/s and 25¢ for handling and mailing to:

PINNACLE BOOKS, INC. / P.O. Box 4347
Grand Central Station / New York, N.Y. 10017

☐ CHECK HERE IF YOU WANT A FREE CATALOG

I have enclosed $_____ check_____ or money order_____
as payment in full. No C.O.D.'s

Name_____

Address_____

City_____ State_____ Zip_____
(Please allow time for delivery)

THE INCREDIBLE ACTION PACKED SERIES

DEATH MERCHANT

by Joseph Rosenberger

His name is Richard Camellion, he's a master of disguise, deception and destruction. He does what the CIA and FBI cannot do. They call him THE DEATH MERCHANT!

Order		Title	Book #	Price
_____	# 1	THE DEATH MERCHANT	P751	$1.25
_____	# 2	OPERATION OVERKILL	P085	.95
_____	# 3	THE PSYCHOTRON PLOT	P641	$1.25
_____	# 4	CHINESE CONSPIRACY	P168	.95
_____	# 5	SATAN STRIKE	P182	.95
_____	# 6	ALBANIAN CONNECTION	P670	$1.25
_____	# 7	CASTRO FILE	P264	.95
_____	# 8	BILLIONAIRE MISSION	P339	.95
_____	# 9	THE LASER WAR	P594	$1.25
_____	#10	THE MAINLINE PLOT	P473	$1.25
_____	#11	MANHATTAN WIPEOUT	P561	$1.25
_____	#12	THE KGB FRAME	P642	$1.25
_____	#13	THE MATO GROSSO HORROR	P705	$1.25